A JOURNEY OF
DESTINY

Patricia Shank Martin

BENCHMARKPRESS
Fixing Our Eyes On Jesus

Benchmark Press
2685 Lime Kiln Road
Chambersburg, PA 17202
benchmarkhymns@gmail.com

ISBN: 978-0-578-81831-3

Layout: M.J. Jacobs LLC - Grand Rapids, MI

Printed in the U.S.A on FSC certified paper

A JOURNEY OF
DESTINY

Patricia Shank Martin

BENCHMARKPRESS

Fixing Our Eyes On Jesus

Foreword

WHAT FIRST COMES TO YOUR MIND when you hear the term "prophet"? Like many people, do you think primarily of a person who foretells the future? A quick look at the writings of the Old Testament will show you that the longest discussions of the prophets were about history. These prophets understood that their people were best prepared to make wise decisions in the present if they had a thorough knowledge of past choices and the consequences of those choices.

Our Anabaptist forefathers have given us a most instructive history and heritage. The precepts that guided their lives have been tested through 500 years of experience. The descendants of these forefathers have responded to their experience in various ways. Their responses also have been tested through the years, and the results have clearly shown the consequences of those responses. Some have kept the Gospel heritage of their forefathers alive for generations to come. But countless others, by playing fast and loose with the precepts of their goodly heritage have doomed their descendants to a worldly caricature of the Gospel. By their careless disregard for the past, they broke a crucial link to the future.

As a mother, my wife, Patricia, wanted her descendants to learn as much wisdom from their family history as possible. A few years ago, she began compiling genealogies and inspirational writings of our family into notebooks for her grandchildren. Her interests have focused particularly on the trials and migrations of her Schenk ancestors as Anabaptists in the Berne area of Switzerland.

In 2017, we traveled to Europe with our daughter, Candace, her husband, Heinrich Schander, and their baby, Camden. For Patricia, our visit to Eggiwil, the town where her Schenk ancestors lived 12 generations ago, was a dream come true. We saw the church building where the Schenks had been baptized in the past. We toured the nearby area of Sumiswald and climbed the stairs of the Trachselwald Castle to see the cells where Hans Hasslebacher, the last Bernese martyr, languished before he was beheaded. We met Hans Hasslebacher, a distant descendant who owns his ancestor's name and farm but not his Anabaptist faith. We contemplated what it meant for 81-year-old Michael Schenk I to tear himself from these idyllic surroundings to make the "endless" trek to the Palatinate with his son, Michael Schenk II, and his family, leaving more than a dozen children behind, together with all his possessions. Why? Because his Anabaptist faith was more important to him than literally anything else in the world.

We came home to ponder our place in a heritage purchased at the cost of everything for God and family. The long journey of Michael Schenk I truly has proved to be "a journey of destiny"! From his very thin family thread have come thousands of my wife's people. A small group of Schenk descendants still practice the faith that Michael Schenk I sacrificed all to possess and pass on to his posterity. For that thin thread of descendants, Patricia has written this story. She sends this book with prayers that none of our family's descendants will break the crucial link to a heritage that once lost will likely never be regained. We urge each of our descendants to read *A Journey of Destiny* and embrace its lessons of hard choices. In doing so, they will experience the Gospel reality of a dearly bought heritage and keep it alive for future generations.

John D. Martin
Chambersburg, Pennsylvania
2 December 2020

Preface

"W HAT'S PAST IS PROLOGUE," proclaims an ancient adage. Our roots set the stage for all of us. Without my ancestral exile from the Swiss Emmental region, I likely would not live in America today. I may have grown up romping Swiss slopes in the Emmental region. Or I may not even exist.

The main characters in this narrative were my ancestors: Michel Schenk I, Michel Schenk II and his wife Anna, and Christian Schenk. Not much is known of their lives. I have filled in details with character and color.

Even though I have no primary source in hand documenting these ancestors' relationship with Christ, at least two evidences point to their Christian faith. The first evidence is their willingness to uproot from an established home in the face of looming religious persecution to undertake a challenging journey together with other Anabaptists to a land of relative religious freedom. The second evidence is the Christian teaching and influence that have rippled down the ages to descendants living in this very day.

A number of years ago my husband and I attended a service in which a representative from the Swiss Reformed people made a public apology for the persecution our historic Anabaptists had received at the hands of the Swiss Reformed state church. John and I were among those who extended our forgiveness. It is the only way forward.

Patricia Shank Martin
Chambersburg, Pennsylvania
December 2020

Acknowledgments

~My highest thanks goes to the Lord Jesus Christ, who is "the way, the truth, and the life" to me.

~Each of my family members have blessed and enriched my life: my beloved husband, John Martin; our daughters and their husbands, Anne and Craig Martin; Heather and Brandon Byler; Candace and Heinrich Schander; our son, Spencer Martin; our grandchildren, Carter, Edward, Charlotte and Elizabeth Martin; Kaitlyn, Hudson and Meghan Byler; Camden and Isaac Schander.

~Many thanks to John, who was my superb in-house editor, who wrote the foreword, and who was an invaluable support to my work.

~Much appreciation goes to Brandon for his fine work on filling in the map as well as his great job on editing some of the manuscript.

~Thank you, Heather, for your valuable content suggestion and encouragement.

~Thanks, Spencer, for giving me wonderful extra household help.

~Heinrich and Candace, thank you for letting John and me share your European journey, along with your baby Camden, in 2017. Heinrich, special thanks for the excursion you gave John and me to the Eggiwil Swiss Reformed church building. My visit to the Eggiwil area greatly enhanced my ancestral connection.

~My brother, Ray Shank, may have done the most to spark my interest in our Schenk ancestry. He originally provided much of the genealogical information I have (see Schenk-Shank Family Ancestry). He has sourced Richard W. Davis, a genealogist (from whom other trickle-down information for my story may derive). Ray also reviewed my basic story and gave me encouragement and helpful advice. Thank you, Ray.

~Many thanks to Mr. Rinck Heule, of M.J. Jacobs, LLC., Grand Rapids, Michigan, who graciously worked with us to bring this book to completion.

Patricia Shank Martin

Contents

Map of Switzerland and Germany

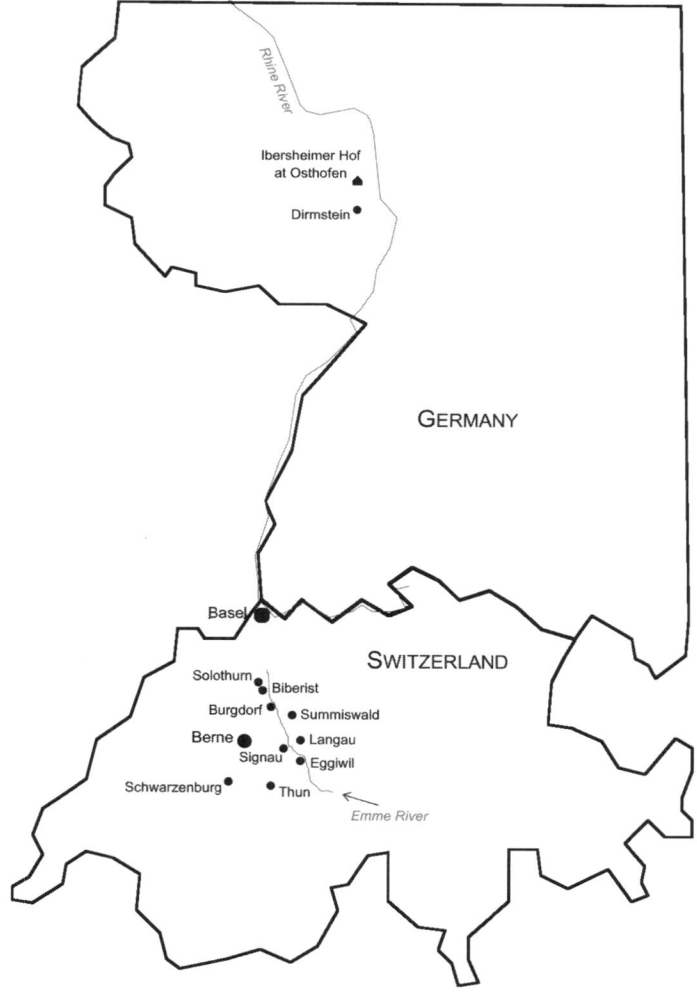

Prologue

*M*ICHEL SCHENK I WATCHED HIS rosy-cheeked grandchildren scamper in the cool air on the hillside of their Swiss home. Sunbeams streamed on their flushed faces as they darted about in play.

Little Barbara chased butterflies, finally grasping one in her hands. She ran over to her grandpapa exclaiming, "Look, Grandpapa, I caught it!" Drawing open her hands slightly, she let him look.

"That's a beautiful butterfly, Barbara!" he told her as he admired its shimmering blue and gold wings.

Christian and his younger brother, Hans, rushed past them, laughing as they raced with each other.

Little Michel III toddled about, picking up twigs and grasping for insects.

The young parents, Michel II and Anna, appeared in the doorway of the chalet and paused, drinking in the beauty of the morning.

For the adults, the tranquility of this day was bitter-sweet, for in only four days they would depart their beloved homeland.

The Emmental region had supplied nourishing soil for the Schenk family tree for many generations. In this year, 1671, their genealogical record had a two-hundred-year span. Young Christian was the son of Michel II, who was the son of Michel I, who was the son of Ulrich, who was the son of Johannes Christian, who was the son of Johannes, who was the son of Hans, who was born in 1470.

Only for Christ would the elder Michel and the young couple uproot and tear themselves away from their home.

Because the government would not permit them to follow the spiritual beliefs and practices dictated by their consciences, persecution threatened them. In Canton Bern, the prescribed church for everyone was the Swiss Reformed Church. Anabaptists found scriptural differences with the state church—such as adult believers' baptism, non swearing of oaths, refusal to defend their native land with weapons, and belief in separation of church and state.

As he considered the rigors of a journey to the German Palatinate in the sunset of his life, Michel also reflected on martyrs of the faith, such as Felix Manz, Michael Sattler, and Hans Haslebacher. Surely he, too, could sacrifice for the sake of Christ.

His eyes caught sight of the beautiful, snow-terraced Hohgant Mountain that had been as constant for him as the soil beneath his feet and the blue sky above his head. Soon he would see the Hohgant no more. But unlike changing scenes of life, the Lord would never change nor fail him.

He thought of the words in Isaiah 54, "For the mountains shall depart, and the hills be removed; but my kindness shall not depart from thee, neither shall the covenant of my peace be removed, saith the Lord that hath mercy on thee."

His reverie was broken when Christian bounded up to him, "Grandpapa, when I'm old, I want to be a Grandpapa just like you! But, first I want to be a Papa just like my papa!"

Grandpapa smiled.

ONE

Shutting the Door

THE MOMENT HER HUSBAND, MICHEL Schenk II, shut the chalet door gently, but firmly behind them, Anna felt that the door of her peaceful life had closed, too. An involuntary shiver ran through her body. The way forward held much uncertainty. As if to confirm her foreboding, a bitter wind suddenly swept across their little family huddled outside the dwelling.

The date was October 16, 1671.

In the faint early morning light, Hans, age six, and Barbara, age four, blinked sleepily as they stood on either side of their mama, Anna. She hugged them closely in the chill wind. The baby, nearly two-year-old Michel III, half dozed on his young papa's arm. Secured on the papa's back and shoulders were two comforters, rolled for convenient travel, which were to suffice for the family bedding on the imminent journey.

Anna gazed longingly at the scene around her. The cozy chalet that had been *home* since her marriage was nestled into the hillside as if it had grown out of the idyllic landscape where it stood. Its overhanging roof and gentle contour beckoned, "Come in, relax, and be comfortable."

Gracing the window boxes that Michel had made for her were late-blooming purple alpine asters, garnered from the nearby mountain. Majestic evergreens stood behind the dwelling. Close at hand, Anna spotted deciduous trees, dressed in autumn colors. Bronze and amber leaves seemed to wave a teary farewell as they stirred in the wind, shaking droplets from last night's rain.

A former scene flashed into her memory. She was standing near this very spot on a beautiful May day about five months before. She and Michel had finished a long discussion about their faith in Christ, their beliefs, and their options for the future. Like a soothing balm, the Lord had assured her that He was her refuge, even as she would surely be a refugee for Him.

And yet, in this early, chilly, wet morning, a surreal sensation crept over her. Was she really leaving the home she had cherished, the land of her birth, never to return?

She felt as if she were grasped by a giant hand and yanked like a pesky weed out of the soil in which she was deeply rooted.

And how about their young and vulnerable children? Were she and Michel needlessly exposing them to danger and possibly death?

Anna saw that their nine-year-old son, Christian, strained with impatience to start down the mountainside. Michel II had warned his son that they would possibly meet danger on this trip. But Christian still hoped for adventure and thrills!

"Maybe we'll meet bears along the way!" And Christian let out a sudden, shrill, "Roar!"

Hans's brown eyes popped wide open. "Bears, papa, will we see bears?"

"Hans," his papa reassured him, "we probably will not see any bears."

"Christian," Michel II cautioned gently, "please be careful what you say."

Christian was more careful this time, "Maybe we will find rabbits. U-m-m, I could eat some rabbit stew!"

Christian had a very important job on this journey. He was to keep a sharp lookout for branches or large stones in the path that might cause his grandpapa, eighty-one-year-old, Michel Schenk I, to stumble and fall. As the two walked together, Christian could call out, "halt," and Grandpapa would know to pause until Christian removed the branch or perhaps led him around a rock.

"Grandpapa, are you excited to start on this trip?" Christian looked eagerly into Grandpapa's face.

Grandpapa was silent for a few moments. Then he smiled lovingly at Christian. "Yes, Christian, I think I can say I am excited. After all, look what wonderful people I will be with—you and your family. But beyond that I believe this is a journey that Jesus wants us to make. It will be exciting to see how the Lord takes care of us on this trip. And this is a journey that will give your papa, mama and me the freedom to serve God and His Kingdom in the way we believe is right. When you are older you may understand this much better."

"Oh," Christian's eyes had a faraway look, "you do have a lot to be excited about."

"Yes, my boy, I've been praying many times a day about this journey."

If all went well, this trek would take this family and others from the Eggiwil community in the Swiss Confederation to the Palatinate in Southwest German territory.

Michel II quietly called his children to attention: "Christian, Hans, Barbara, Michel, it is time to pray."

Briefly Michel thanked the Lord for His mercy in their lives to that point. He prayed that God would give strength to Grandpapa, a careful and obedient spirit to Christian, kind and loving actions to Hans and Barbara, happiness to baby Michel, comfort to his dear wife, wisdom to himself, and safety for them all.

At last, the procession formed to head down the steep slope. Grandpapa and Christian were in the lead, Anna followed with Hans and Barbara, and Michel carried little Michel.

Michel's prayer was like salve on a wound. Still, after a last lingering look at the home she had cherished, unbidden tears crept to the surface and slid down Anna's cheeks.

"Lord, I am willing," Anna prayed silently, "I am willing to face today with its partings. And when tomorrow comes, I will face that day because You are with me."

– TWO –

Georg and Elsbeth

*H*UES OF SOFT ROSE, MAUVE AND RED painted the morning sky as the small caravan began its descent into the valley. The pair leading the way was having a grand time together.

Quick as a wink, Christian whisk a large branch out of Grandpapa's way.

"The wind I heard whistling about must have taken down quite a number of branches," observed Grandpapa as Christian moved ahead clearing the path. Like a bee buzzing from one flower to the next, Christian whizzed from one branch to the next.

"Christian, my boy, I think I am getting dizzy with all your flying about," Grandpapa smiled. "And you know what can happen to people when they get dizzy?" he grinned.

Christian laughed, "They can fall down!"

"Grandpapa, tell me a story," Christian begged, "about when you were a boy."

"Ah, yes," Grandpapa leaned against his cane and gazed into the streaks of rosy light announcing the new day, "a story from my childhood . . ." he mused.

"Yes, I remember something that happened when I was probably about the age you are now."

Christian spotted a rock jutting up in the path, "Grandpapa, halt, halt!" he yelled.

The young boy tried to pry the rock loose, but it was imbedded in the ground and wouldn't budge. "Here, let me take your hand, Grandpapa, and I'll guide you around the rock."

"As I said, I was probably about the age you are now," Grandpapa said.

"Grandpapa, can you tell me the story, too?" Hans wanted to listen in.

"Me, too?" joined in little Barbara.

"Certainly, my little ones. Just come a little closer so I don't have to talk so loudly."

Anna drew the two children forward a little.

"One day my mama found out that our neighbor man and his wife, far up the mountain, had not been doing well as they had been ill and had no children to take care of them," Grandpapa's story began.

"'Ulrich', she said to my papa, 'Would you please take soup I have prepared and some fresh bread to Georg and Elsbeth Egli'?"

"'Yes, Annali, give me time to milk the cow and then

I should be on my way'."

"As a young boy I was like you, Christian. I jumped at the chance to add something fun and exciting to my day. So I begged my papa, 'I could help you carry the food, Papa. May I go along'?

"My papa looked at my mama. 'What do you think, Annali'?

"'You do need someone to help you carry the food, and Michel has finished his chores. So, yes, that would work fine'.

"'Michel', my mama added, 'be quiet, as these are elderly people and have not been well. You need to be careful not to make them feel worse'."

"'Oh, I will be very quiet, Mama', I assured her.

"By the time my papa and I started our trek up the steep mountainside, the afternoon was slipping away. Papa took long and fast steps, and I ran to keep up.

"When my papa knocked on their chalet door, a booming voice called out, 'Who comes'?

"My papa boomed back, 'Ulrich Schenk, with food for you'.

"'If your name is Schenk, do come in', the voice hollered.

"My papa carefully opened the door and placed the soup on the table, motioning for me to do the same with the bread. I saw a large man sitting at the table. When he talked, his voice filled the whole house."

"Grandpapa, why did the man talk so loudly?" wondered Christian.

"Maybe to hear himself talk!" Grandpapa reasoned.

"Georg asked, 'Why Ulrich Schenk, what brings you here on this November day? It is mighty good to see you! And what is your name, my boy'?

"Of course, I remembered my mama's instruction to be quiet. So I said softly, 'Michel'.

"'Say it again, my boy', Georg yelled.

"'Michel', I said, a little louder this time.

"'Michel'! my papa boomed.

"'That's a mighty good name, my boy'.

"Georg's wife was a small lady, whose face was wreathed in smiles as she spoke, 'Thank you for the soup. It will taste wonderful on this chilly evening. We have not been feeling well these past days. But I do believe Georg has perked up some since you are here'.

"'Ah, it makes a man feel better just to see some visitors. My wife already knows all my stories, but now that you are here, I get a chance to have a listening ear'.

"'Georg, did you grow up in this chalet'? my papa inquired.

"'Yes, I've lived here all my life. I like it up here. The further up the mountain a person lives, it seems the closer he is to God. Of course, people in the valley can be just as close to God', he smiled. Then he sighed and continued, 'We've certainly needed the Lord'. And here Georg stopped and a tear rolled down his cheek. 'It's been fifty years since our small twin boys drowned in the rushing stream. They were all we had. But the Lord was good to me. Elsbeth is the apple of my eye. When I first saw her I knew she was the one for me. It took quite a while for me to convince her papa to let me marry her. After all, she was the oldest child in her family, and he needed her help on the farm. Besides, she was quite young. So when I asked her papa if I could marry her, he said it wasn't the time, yet. I waited four years, and by then, he had other children old enough to help. It was a happy day when I could marry my Elsbeth'.

"Georg's voice never abated. And Elsbeth seemed to never stop smiling.

"Georg's stories went on and on. Finally, my papa realized we had to leave hurriedly, so he grabbed a moment to speak, 'Annali may wonder if we have lost our way'! Papa quipped with a grin.

"Imagine our shock upon opening the chalet door to go home, and finding it had been softly snowing. Soon the snowfall gathered strength and pelted us, piling rapidly on the path. All we saw ahead was whiteness. Besides our own footsteps, all we heard was the wind, which stirred the snow in eddies around us.

"Finally Papa spoke in a husky voice, 'Michel, I have lost my way! With the snow and darkness, I don't see anything familiar'.

"It was a moment of truth for me. I was totally shocked to hear my Papa tell me he didn't know how to do something! It was just natural for him to figure out how to do everything he tried to do.

"I can picture the scene in my mind to this very day. My papa raised his arms high toward the heavens, with snow pelting on his upturned face. He clasped his hands and beseeched the Lord in a most direct manner."

And here Grandpapa Michel demonstrated with upraised and clasped hands the posture his own papa had used.

"And this is what he prayed, 'Lord, my son Michel and I are lost. If it pleases You, guide us safely home. For the glory of God and in the name of Jesus, Amen'.

"The wind cut through our coats, but I was shivering as much from fright as from the cold," Grandpapa remembered.

"Still, my papa stood quietly with his hands clasped and raised high toward the heavens. Finally, he spoke, 'Michel, I believe this is the way to go'.

"By this time, it was difficult to walk in the deep snow. We veered to the left, according to Papa's direction from the Lord, and we carefully made our way down the steep incline. Yes! I could faintly see a building in the distance. On and on we went until I knew it was our chalet!

"When we finally pushed open our door, and I got a glimpse of Mama's face, I almost cried because she looked so worried!

"Papa said soothingly, 'It's all right, Annali. The Lord took care of us, didn't He, Michel'?

"I could hardly speak, but when I caught my breath, I explained, 'Yes, Papa raised his hands like this', and I showed how he had done it, 'And he asked the Lord if it pleased Him, to bring us safely home. And He did'."

"Grandpapa," Christian was in awe, "I'm sure glad your papa found the way home."

"Never forget, my boy, it was the Lord that brought us home safely. My papa just listened to the Lord!"

- THREE -

A Journey of Destiny

INALLY, THE SCHENK FAMILY reached the town of Eggiwil. They walked past the Swiss Reformed church building. Dating from 1631, the building housed the "baptismal" records of many Emmental babies, including Michel and Anna's own children. She remembered each christening date: Christian received the rite on June 15, 1662, Hans on December 4, 1664, Barbara on April 14, 1667, and Michel III on January 4, 1670.

As parents of newborns, Michel and Anna had struggled to know whether to obey the mandate of the Canton Bern to take their babies to receive the sacrament of "infant baptism" administered by the parish minister. Should they risk disobedience to the state authority?

In the end, their conviction that "infant baptisms" were not true baptisms was one reason they decided to depart this land. Since Scripture says, "He that believeth and is baptized shall be saved," they knew that only those who were old enough to repent of their sinful life and follow Christ could enter His Kingdom by baptism.

As other Swiss Brethren assembled, Anna saw that the Hans Roet and the Hans Schneider families were two other families with young children making the journey. This could provide interesting times, she thought! And it would be special for her two older boys to have other children on the journey.

When the minister, Christian Stauffer, Anna's paternal grandpapa, saw that all the refugees were assembled, he spoke to the group.

"Brothers and sisters in Christ, I greet you this momentous day as a fellow citizen of the Kingdom of God. All the adult emigrants in this assembly have received baptism upon confession of their faith in Jesus Christ and are relying on His blood for the cleansing of their sins. All of you believers seek also to build Christ's Kingdom on this earth.

"I have spoken to you all and am gratified that as part of Christ's body, we all subscribe to the following Scriptural teachings:

"We believe that Christians need to follow Him as their conscience dictates, and so the church and state should be separate.

Because only those who believe and are baptized can be part of Christ's Kingdom, we subscribe to adult baptism.

Jesus calls us not to swear, so we will not take an oath. We will not kill human life, which includes bearing arms to defend the state.

Only those who voluntarily choose to follow Christ are worthy to be considered part of His church.

Our purpose is to follow Jesus' teaching in loving our enemies, letting our light shine, and forgiving others."

The Schenks knew that many in Eggiwil sympathized with them as Anabaptists, but either didn't have the convictions they did or didn't have the courage to leave as they were doing.

The village minister noted their imminent departure and gave them an amiable wave as they walked past the church building.

Anna's Grandpapa Stauffer called on Michel Schenk II to lead in a parting prayer.

"Our kind Father in heaven," Michel prayed, "may your name be hallowed among us. May we as Christians represent Your kingdom on this earth and may your will be done here as in heaven. In all our actions, help us to live and to show others the way of Christ.

"We ask for food for each day's need.

"With the spirit of Jesus, help us to forgive those who oppose us, as also we ask You to forgive our sins.

"Deliver us from temptation and evil and from the

power of the Evil One.

"For our elderly and our little ones, we ask for Your special grace and kindness during the rigors of this trip.

"And Father," here Michel's voice broke. When he composed himself he continued, "I believe this is a journey of destiny. So, as we step forward may the results of our action today ripple down the ages for Your glory. Stir the hearts of our children and ongoing generations to follow the Lord Jesus and to take their own steps of faith, always for Christ and for His kingdom.

"Father in heaven, Yours is the kingdom, the power, and the glory now and forever. Amen in the name of Jesus Christ."

Anna's eyes were glistening with tears when Michel finished the prayer. Never had she felt so responsible to show her children the way of Christ as she did now.

– FOUR –

Walking Together

$\mathcal{N}$OW IT WAS TIME FOR THE EMI-
grants to line up in order. The frontward
scouts were two single men in their twen-
ties, Hans Stauffer and Ulrich Stauffer. Next came Anna's
paternal grandpapa, Christian Stauffer, and the lady he
had married after his first wife died.

The refugees found their places as assigned by the
scouts. The rearward scouts were Peter Bachman, and
Ulrich Liecte, who was waiting for his wife and children
to come later.

Just ahead of Michel I and his grandson, Christian,
walked the Hans Roet family. Christian was ecstatic! He
and Hans had become fast friends with the young boys
in the Roet family, Heinrich and Niklaus.

Anna could see the excitement building on her son's
countenance. "Mama," he whispered, his face all smiles,
"Heinrich's family is just ahead of us. Won't we have fun?"

Anna recalled the day more than a year ago when the Hans Roet family came to visit them. While the men discussed spiritual matters and how to respond to pressure from the authorities, she and Margareta also talked about their convictions.

Meanwhile, the ladies heard shouting from outside the chalet as one of the boys hollered, "I caught you! Now it's my turn to hide!"

"Would you like to sit outside where we can keep an eye on the children?" Anna suggested.

"That's an excellent plan," Margareta agreed. "If your boys are as full of ideas as mine, things may get pretty interesting!" And Margareta laughed as she rolled her eyes.

The women found their voices almost drowned out with the laughter and hilarity of the children. The boys ran races, jumped over fallen tree limbs and turned summersaults until their faces were crimson.

Christian must have decided it was time for a quieter game, as he suggested that they play, "Thinking of Something."

"Are you ready?" Christian asked. "I'm thinking of something."

Soon "playing quietly" escalated into a noisy game as well.

Now the Roets and the Schenks would be close together on the trek! Anna returned Christian's exuberant smile! Rarely did the older children have a chance to play with other children, and this would be special to have playmates on the long journey.

The first day of walking was tiring for everyone, even those who were accustomed to traipsing up and down the Emmental slopes.

Little Michel grew weary of his ride on his papa's strong arm. "Papa, Papa, down! Michel get down," he begged.

His papa put him down, held his little hands and let him take some steps. Soon he scooped the little one into his arms again.

Someone started a hymn, and soon many others joined in the singing. Michel's little voice punctuated the melody with his unintelligible syllables.

The caravan planned to follow the beautiful, blue waters of the Emme River as it flowed northward until they were near Solothurn. Anna felt as if she were one of the Israelites drinking of the water gushing from the rock when Michel brought his family cold, refreshing water from the Emme.

Anna admired her husband's uncle, Christian Schenk, who, at age ninety-five was willing to make this trek. Michel II kindly asked him how he was doing in keeping up with the walking pace of others in the caravan.

"The Lord is still giving me strength to follow Him," said Uncle Christian as he leaned on his cane and smiled while taking the next step.

– FIVE –

Terror Meets Gentle

THE NEXT MORNING MICHEL SCHENK I gave a Scripture testimony he had been asked to share.

"Brothers and sisters in Christ," the elderly gentleman began, "I want to turn our attention to the Shepherd of Psalm 23."

And here he quoted the Psalm, "'The Lord is my shepherd . . .' Now, more than ever before, the Shepherd who leads me is not only my Guide, my Protector, and my Provider, but He is also the Lord of the New Testament—He is my Saviour and my Friend.

"As a struggling young Papa I knew what it meant to work hard and yet to worry about providing for my wife and growing family. In time, I learned to rest in the Shepherd's care. I worked as hard as ever, but worry left me because I realized that the Shepherd would see to our needed provision.

"I learned also that my spiritual needs and those of my family were a priority, so I studied Scripture, listened to godly men preach, and observed the lives of those who were at peace and following the Shepherd. That convinced me, too, to become a sheep in the Shepherd's flock.

"As He supplied the green pastures for our lodging last night, beside the refreshing Emme River, so He provides the refreshment of rest spiritually when we follow Him.

"He did indeed lead me in a right path when I cried out to Him. I had tried to lead a godly life, but I didn't know what 'repentance' meant. When I saw that repentance was turning from the 'me' and my sinful desires and surrendering to Him, it made sense, because the 'me' was on a failing course. I looked to the Saviour, my Shepherd, who not only said, 'follow Me' but also cleansed my sinful past with His blood and empowered me to live in a right way, in righteousness.

"But brothers and sisters, last night as I lay on the hard ground wrapped in my comforter, I was also wrapped in fear. I was in fear for your lives and my own. I was in fear of the rigors of the trip, I was in fear of our enemies, and I was in fear of death. My heart was throbbing with utter desolation. I felt the darkness of death. I saw no light, no Shepherd to lead me out of that midnight terror. It seemed as if the Lord had utterly abandoned me. Finally, my heart cried out, 'The Lord is my Shepherd'!"

"Then the Lord opened my mind to see clearly what was happening. My good Shepherd said, 'Resist the devil, and he will flee from you. Draw nigh to God, and he will draw nigh to you'. So I told the devil he had to leave because the good Shepherd had given His life to save me from the doom and destruction that the devil was wrapping around me. And I reminded the devil that Christ's blood had washed me clean and that he couldn't keep company with a sheep and his Shepherd. It was only my Shepherd's presence that gave me courage to withstand the devil in this manner.

"Then my Shepherd did prepare a table of wonderful blessings for me as this scripture came to mind, 'He brought me to the banqueting house, and his banner over me was love'.

"It reminded me of the time, years ago, when we had young children and my wife was sick. Times were hard, food was scarce, but my wife was too ill to prepare what we did have. Unexpectedly, an Anabaptist lady and her husband appeared at our door and brought soup, bread and cheese. It tasted like kings' delicacies!

"At the same time the Shepherd fed me with spiritual food, He anointed my wounds with oil and filled my cup to overflowing. The kindness of this Anabaptist couple led me to study their beliefs. Now here I am today.

"Together my dear fellow Christians, we need not fear physical death if the *Shepherd* is with us. He leads us to our new, *safe* home—His home."

After prayer for the continued presence of the Good Shepherd, Grandpapa also blessed the food they had carried with them for the morning.

Michel II lead in a hymn written by an Anabaptist, Balthasar Hubmaier:

"Rejoice, rejoice, ye Christians all, and break forth into singing!
Since far and wide on ev'ry side the Word of God is ringing.
And well ye know, no human foe our souls from Christ can sever;
For to the base and men of grace, God's Word stands sure forever."

The Ulrich Eymann family had brought with them a cow, named *Gentle*. With each milking, Ulrich kindly shared her milk with all the children. Then the adults drank milk by turns.

Michel II took out a little food from the provision they had brought along and shared some with each member of his family. Anna noted that he kept only a small portion of bread and a tiny piece of cheese for himself. She broke off a piece of her own cheese. "Michel, the baby didn't drink all of his milk, and I finished it. So take this," she urged.

Michel hesitated, but Anna insisted. "What an unselfish husband!" she contemplated.

The morning trek had barely begun when a ferocious snarl split the air. A wild dog with bared teeth and malicious eyes sprang at the caravan. Children screamed, papas and mamas clutched their little ones, and the elderly froze in their tracks. The four scouts whirled about snatching up fallen branches as they rushed to head off the mongrel. They skillfully swung their sticks, keeping the savage dog at bay. The mongrel tried a new tactic. He stood plastered to the ground, then he hunkered down, growling, eyes shooting fire.

"His name is *Terror*," quipped Heinrich Roet, laughing nervously.

"Yeah, it sure is," agreed Christian, with a shaky chuckle.

The Ulrich Eymann family with Gentle, the cow, stood at the back of the caravan, unprotected by the scouts who were surrounding Terror.

Terror slyly aimed his sights on Gentle. Making a wild dash toward the cow, he jumped at her side, trying to sink his teeth into her belly. Although it was a failed attempt, Gentle was not amused. When Terror leaped into the air and lunged at her again, Gentle's hoof whizzed into defensive mode, landing squarely on the mongrel's stomach.

Silence reigned for a moment. Then came a high-pitched, mournful yelping.

Heinrich, Niklaus, Christian, and Hans doubled over with laughter, and their nervousness gave way to howling as they watched Terror slinking into the thicket, tail between his legs.

"What do I see?" Michel II muttered, looking toward the west where the town of Signau lay. Two men on horseback were headed their way. One of the scouts sent a muffled alert through the crowd. A hush descended and Anna sensed that many were praying as she was.

She and Michel watched the approaching riders closely.

Anna was shocked and puzzled when she saw their clothing. Large hats with drooping plumes!? Shabby red coats with worn brass buttons . . .? outsized pants?

Had these clothes been lying in an ancient chest for a century or two?

She decided they could be officials, perhaps bailiffs, trying to look important.

Her ears perked up instantly when one of the bailiffs barked, "What is meant by all this commotion?" His voice dripped with contempt.

"We are peaceable folk passing through this area. Suddenly a wild dog tried to harm us," Christian Stauffer meekly replied.

"A likely story," spat out the second bailiff as he tossed his head, further endangering his drooping plume.

"What a ludicrous spectacle he makes," thought Anna.

"We think you are Anabaptists trying to hide from the authorities. We know of a fine castle with a dungeon, which would provide housing for you all," spoke the first bailiff.

Like lightening, Terror crashed from the thicket and tore up to the bailiff who had threatened the Anabaptists. Sinking his sharp teeth into the rider's leg, Terror managed to bite twice before one of the scouts chased him away. A look of pain crossed the injured man's face.

"As we have matters to attend to in the village, we must be going now," the second bailiff remarked.

Just as their horses pranced away, Anna noticed blood dripping from the first bailiff's wounded leg.

"Behold, the Terror of the Lord," Michel I observed wryly.

- SIX -

Blessed Are the Little Feet

MICHEL BOUNCED THE BABY gently up and down, up and down, to keep himself awake as he walked. It was a drowsy time of the afternoon.

Anna's hands were unpleasantly warm and moist from holding Hans's and Barbara's little hands. But the children might fall asleep if she did not help them move forward.

"My feet hurt," whimpered Barbara.

"Let Mama carry you for a little while," Anna replied soothingly.

"But I'm a *big* girl now!" Barbara was indignant.

"Of course, you are a big girl! But sometimes even big girls need a little help. And since your feet hurt, I could carry you for a little while," Anna offered.

"But I'm too big," asserted Barbara.

"Lord, this is a problem for you to solve," thought Anna. Finally, she told Barbara, "I am sorry your feet hurt. Shall we tell Papa about it?"

Barbara nodded dolefully. A tear slid down her cheek.

When Papa heard about Barbara's feet, he gave a low whistle to stop the train of people. Then he handed the baby to Anna and knelt down on one knee while he balanced Barbara on the other knee.

"My little one, let me see your feet." He removed one shoe and tapped the end of her big toe. "Does that hurt, Barbara?" Again, she nodded. He compared her foot with the bottom of her shoe. Ah! This was a problem. The shoes were pinching her big toes.

He looked at his wife, "She has outgrown her shoes," Michel said slowly, pondering a solution.

Dismay clouded Anna's brown eyes. Her mind spun . . . embarrassment and shame throbbed through her brain.

"Why Michel, I should have noticed that her shoes no longer fit her! That pair was given to us by my brother's family. Of course, they have three girls in a row, all older than Barbara. She was so happy with these shoes that had belonged to her cousins. And being the *big* girl that she is, she wanted to put the shoes on herself. She would tug and tug until she finally pulled on each shoe. I wasn't keeping track, and of course I didn't notice that her feet had outgrown her shoes. . ." Anna's voice trailed off limply.

"I am so sorry, Barbara," her mama apologized. "I should have been thinking about your feet growing too big for these shoes!" Anna's face was flushed and her heart raced. What would they do for Barbara now?

"Don't worry, Anna, I have an idea," Michel told her. "But let's pray about it first."

"Barbara, let's pray about your feet that hurt," her papa told her gently. So Michel prayed, "Lord, Barbara's feet hurt because her shoes are too small. Help us to solve the problem."

Michel drew a small knife from his pocket, took Barbara's shoe in hand and painstakingly removed stitching from the toe area of each shoe.

Then he put the shoes on Barbara's feet. "Now stand up, Barbara," he said as he helped her to her feet.

"Wiggle your toes around a little. Do you think your feet will feel better now?"

Barbara looked up and smiled, "That feels better. Thank you, Papa."

"You are welcome, my girl."

Then a little frown appeared on her face. "But nobody else has toes sticking out of their shoes," she whined.

"Barbara," her papa comforted her, "with your stockings on, nobody will see your bare toes. Keep thinking about how much better your feet feel with room for your toes to spread out!"

Here mama chimed in, "Did you know, Barbara, the Bible talks about beautiful feet? I hope all our feet become lovely in the way the Bible talks about them in this Scripture, 'How beautiful are the feet of them that preach the gospel of peace, and bring glad tidings of good things'. Using our feet to go and tell people about Jesus makes our feet beautiful!"

Barbara looked down at her big toes sticking out from her open-toed shoes as if to find beautiful feet.

"Jesus loved young children like you, Barbara," her mama continued. "He said, 'Suffer little children, and forbid them not, to come unto me; for of such is the kingdom of heaven.'"

Barbara looked up at mama, took her hand, and smiled.

– SEVEN –

Anna's Dream

THE LARGE COMFORTER WAS BARELY big enough for Michel, Anna, and all their children to have under and over them as they slept on the ground, but it had kept them warm.

Now crisp weather had arrived in earnest. Michel anticipated a frost as the family settled in for the night.

But Anna's mind turned to something more urgent than cold autumn weather. For the evening meal, Michel and Anna had given Grandpapa and the children most of the remaining bread and cheese. Even so, every member of the family was still hungry when the meal was finished.

Little Michel had cried, "Bread, Papa, bread, please," waving his hands toward Papa. Hans and Barbara had looked longingly toward Papa but said nothing. Christian had simply looked away.

Recently, Gentle had produced much less milk than she had at the first. So this evening each child had only a little milk, with none left for the adults.

Anna thought of the little bag of Reichsthaler coins that Michel had hidden in an inside pocket of his shirt. It wasn't much money, but enough for now.

The brethren planned to send the four scouts into the nearby village early in the morning to buy bread at an inn. Michel and others had given money for the bread.

Now as Anna lay on the hard ground, she tried to *will* herself asleep. But hunger gnawed at her stomach so persistently sleep would not come.

Then, like a soothing blanket, she sensed the presence of the Lord surrounding her. "Commit thy way unto the Lord; trust also in him; and he shall bring it to pass." Her heart and her whole being claimed the promise of this Scripture when she realized that instead of trusting God for the family's food needs, she was worrying. As she lay in a sleepy daze, she kept committing, over and over, her family's needs to the Lord.

In her dream, Anna saw Michel smiling and walking toward her. His six-foot frame and broad shoulders bespoke strength. His blue eyes were as firm and steady as Emmental Alps. But it was his Christian commitment that defined him. She saw Michel as he truly was—a man set to live by his conscience, informed by the Word of God. Following Christ was his sincere goal. With courage in his heart he faced the difficulty of the day.

Anna dreamed of their beautiful wedding day, September 21, 1660.

A light rain had fallen followed by the most vivid

rainbow Anna had ever seen. As she and Michel walked toward the parish church building in Eggiwil, they saw a complete rainbow span as well.

"God's radiant gift to us," Michel had murmured.

"Yes, it seems as if He is showing us He will be faithful to us all of our lives," Anna had replied. The sun had beamed down on them as if in celebration of this special day. As if in a dream, they had stepped through the doorway of the church building. Their trust in God and in one another was unswerving. And when they had promised their lives to one another before God and the parish minister, their cup of happiness was overflowing. Their parents and brothers and sisters showered them with love and well wishes. A marvelous wedding feast was prepared by the families, and Michel and Anna had basked in the joy and beauty of this momentous day.

Suddenly Anna was roused from her dreamy flight into the past. In her semi-awakened state, she heard a twig snap and saw a faint movement among the trees.

"Michel," she whispered, "Michel." But he didn't awaken. Anna's heart beat fast and fear gripped her. Finally, with faint moon light she saw a slender four-legged creature walk past their huddled family. It looked like a deer, not a bear. And then another deer. Her body relaxed and she fell into a deep sleep.

- EIGHT -

The Lord is my Shepherd

HE SCOUTS HAD STARTED OUT WELL before dawn to purchase the needed bread. Anna was awake and saw them slip away into the darkness. "Oh, Lord," she prayed, "protect them with your strong arm. Help them to find an inn with enough bread to feed all of our hungry people."

Before streaks of light colored the morning sky, many of the refugees had roused and sat eagerly awaiting their anticipated breakfast.

Ulrich Eymann milked the cow. Again, Gentle produced a scanty supply of milk. Again, each child drank a small portion.

Over and over, Michel II and others walked to the bank of the Emme River and brought back cold water for their families and friends. Anna found it impossible to drink much, because the water made her cold body feel even colder.

And where were the scouts?

Damp air seeped through the refugees' coats. Gray clouds hung low in the humid air.

Eyes turned expectantly when someone spotted four figures in the distance. Bread at last!

The scouts quickly distributed the bread. "We didn't want any inn keeper getting suspicious about us, so we bought only some of the bread at Langnau. At the next town we left one of our scouts hidden in the thicket to guard the bread while three of us went into the inn and bought more bread," explained Peter Bachman.

Michel II and others thanked them heartily for the bread they had wisely purchased.

Hans Roet led in blessing God for the wonderful bread.

Baby Michel held out his little hands, "Bread," he laughed. Michel II quickly broke pieces of bread for his family members. Little Michel would have stuffed his mouth full if his mama had allowed it. Instead, she broke off small portions and gave them to him as he was able to chew it. Barbara, Hans, and Christian took their bread with eager hands and soon it was gone.

Hans Roet stood up to speak. "What have most of us been thinking about more than anything else?" he asked.

"Bread!" one of the brethren answered.

"Yes, bread is uppermost in my mind when I awake in the morning, and bread seems like an elusive dream when I go to sleep at night.

"When my children look to me with hunger in their eyes, it is one of the hardest things I have to face as a papa. When I realize that my wife is sacrificing some of her bread so that the rest of us can have a little more, it hurts my heart.

"Jesus taught his disciples to pray, 'Give us this day our daily bread'. We have asked, and although our bread has not been plentiful, thanks be to God, He has answered our prayer.

"But Jesus also said, 'Man shall not live by bread alone, but by every word that proceedeth out of the mouth of God'. The bread Jesus is talking about forever satisfies the longing of our spirits, as He says, 'I am the bread of life: he that cometh to me shall never hunger; and he that believeth on me shall never thirst'.

"This morning we ate delicious, freshly baked, life-giving bread! It satisfied the hunger pangs of our physical bodies. But soon we will need more.

"But the bread that Jesus spoke about is an everlasting bread, fully satisfying to our spirits if we keep following Him. So may we say with those of old, 'Lord, evermore give us this bread'."

Hans then offered prayer, thanking the Lord for both physical bread and spiritual bread, and beseeching His continued mercy for their journey.

Michel II led in this hymn stanza:

"Touch, Lord, the lips that speak for Thee; Set words of truth before us,

That we may grow in constancy, The light of wisdom o'er us,

*Give us this day our daily bread; May hungry souls
again be fed;*
May heav'nly food restore us."

Christian watched as his papa rolled their family's large comforter. Then Michel II rolled Grandpapa's smaller comforter.

"Papa," Christian said timidly, "I think I could carry Grandpapa's comforter on my back. That way you won't have to take both of them."

Michel II looked quizzically at his son. In Christian's face he saw excitement and a beginning manliness. "Christian, that's great of you to offer," he said with a smile. "So if you think you can carry this one, I'll attach it to your back and shoulders, my young man," he said as he placed the comforter on Christian's back.

"Mama," whispered Christian, "Papa called me young man!"

"Why yes, that's what you are, Christian, because you have been so kind and helpful to Grandpapa," said his mama.

Anna thought the boy surely bore a resemblance to young David in Saul's armor! But she kept her smile to herself until Christian was looking the other way. Then she and Michel gave each other knowing winks.

Christian stepped into procession with his head held high and a strut in his step. Although the comforter was rolled as tightly as her husband could manage, Anna saw that it still dragged on the ground a bit as Christian walked. It bothered her a little. "But he needs to feel useful in this way," she thought.

Grandpapa glanced at Christian. He opened his mouth to say something, then he closed it and walked on in silence.

Soon Grandpapa smiled at Christian, "Thank you, my boy, for carrying my comforter! It would be a bit too heavy for an old man like I am. And it does give your papa a break."

Christian attempted to stand even taller. "Oh, y-es, Grand-pa-pa!" he huffed, his face red from exertion, "I want to do some-thing to he-lp."

Anna's reverie brought her thoughts back to the subject of bread. "Lord, you have always provided for our needs," she prayed silently. "Thank you for giving our hungry children bread this morning. Thank you for the lesson on spiritual bread. Help me to focus on your life-giving salvation when I feel discouraged. Thank you for this wonderful group of Christians with whom to share the perils of the journey and a little part of Christ's Kingdom here on earth. Thank you for my godly husband who is blessed with wisdom and spiritual insight to guide me and our family. Thank you for Grandpapa and his amazing spiritual stability and his willingness to make this journey, in the face of older age. Thank you for our precious children. Lord, I commit their future into Your powerful hands."

The group walked along for some time in silence. Then Anna saw Grandpapa start to sway. But her husband had seen it, too. He was still holding the baby, but he held out his free arm to catch his papa. Anna reached for the baby so Michel could carefully place his papa on the ground.

Her heart thumped. What was happening? Had exhaustion overtaken him? Perhaps he was weak from insufficient food. Was he dying?

Anna and the children stayed out of the way so Michel could care for his papa.

"Papa, papa, are you all right?" Michel inquired softly.

But his papa made no response.

Michel took his wrist and felt for a pulse.

He looked gravely at Anna, "He has a pulse, but it is weak."

"Please pray, Anna," Michel begged.

"Oh yes," she breathed. And in her desperation Anna pleaded with the Lord to be with her husband's papa, and if it pleased the Lord, to raise him up again.

Meanwhile a group of brothers gathered around and begin to pray.

Michel II held his papa's hand and continued to feel for his pulse. He could feel a pulse, but it stayed weak.

Suddenly Christian could stand it no longer. He broke away from his spot beside his mama, rushed up and knelt down beside his grandpapa and cried, "Oh, Grandpapa, please don't die yet!"

He rubbed his grandpapa's cheek and stroked his hair.

Grandpapa's eyelids flickered and he weakly raised his hand. "Christian, my young man," he said faintly. And then Michel II and Christian heard him whisper, "Michel, the Lord is my shepherd."

"Yes, Papa," Michel told him, "the Lord is your shepherd. Many of us are praying for you." He squeezed his papa's hand.

"What am I hearing?" thought Anna, a sudden fear racing through her mind. The emigrants were a bit secluded among the trees. But a horse-drawn cart had found its way to them. A man jumped out of the cart and strode over to the group.

"I saw a number of people here and thought I would see if we could help in some way." The man seemed to have chosen his words carefully.

Anna's mind raced. "Can we trust these men? Will they turn us over to strange authorities, even though the Eggiwil minister knew we were leaving the land?"

But Michel II was already calmly explaining, "My elderly papa was weak and started to fall. Now he seems to be reviving a little. But," and here Michel paused, "we can hardly continue our journey right now."

Everything became quiet.

The stranger looked around. "You have no horse or cart?"

"We do not," Michel answered quietly.

"It will take a bit of time, but he needs to come and rest at our place until he is better." The stranger was planning rapidly, "I will take you along with your papa," he said to Michel II. "And the rest of your group can follow my son, Daniel, as he leads the way toward our place. We have room to lodge you all for the night. My name is

Jakob Kohler," he concluded.

Here was a man of decisive action, for sure. Anna wondered what his wife would think when the cart rolled in with an ailing man and his son, later to be followed by a group of roughly fifty people! All for overnight lodging!

But maybe this was a trap. This would be a good one. Without much effort, the authorities could apprehend a large group of Anabaptist believers with 'one drag of the net'.

"'The Lord is my shepherd' too," thought Anna.

– NINE –

Hospitality

WITH LITTLE MICHEL IN HER ARMS, Anna gathered her other children around her. It felt strange, starting off without her husband.

But Daniel Kohler, the young man assigned by his papa to lead them, must be "a chip off the old block" she thought, because he was already stepping forward rapidly. Her children were half running to keep up, and Anna could see that the pace was too fast for the elderly also. One of the scouts kindly ask young Daniel if he could slow down a bit because of the elderly and young children.

Daniel was apologetic, "I'm sorry, I wasn't thinking about them. I was just on my way home," he chuckled. Anna decided that he was a likable fellow, just thoughtless.

She instructed Christian to hold hands with Hans and Barbara and help them along. Christian was still carrying Grandpapa's comforter on his back. But he seemed to have caught his stride, because he wasn't huffing anymore.

Then Anna felt a slight tap on her shoulder. She turned to see Hans Schneider's wife, Katharina, smiling timidly at her.

"I could carry little Michel for a while if that would help you," she offered.

Anna thought of protesting, but she checked herself when she saw the longing in Katharina's eyes. And a sudden memory flashed into her mind. Katharina's baby had died about seven months ago. He had been born not long after little Michel.

She carefully handed over her little one, who was sleeping by now. Smiling warmly, she thanked Katharina.

Peter Bachman, a rearward scout came forward. "Would Christian like me to carry the comforter now?" he asked.

"Christian," Anna said, "Peter is kindly offering to carry the comforter now. Do you think that would be a good idea?"

Christian looked at Peter, relief flooding his eyes. "Yes, thank you, Peter."

"Thank you, Lord," Anna prayed silently. "I miss my husband. But the 'Body of Christ' stepped up to help."

Sometime later, the squeaky wheels of a cart could be heard. Jakob Kohler reappeared with his cart. But then, Anna saw a second, a third, and even a fourth cart! The young men driving these carts were probably Jakob's sons, she thought.

Jakob wanted the elderly to have rides, so Christian

Stauffer and Christian Schenk, Michel II's uncle, were among those helped into the carts.

Anna did her best to encourage her children, "Soon maybe we can see how Grandpapa is doing and be with Papa again."

Christian smiled shyly at his mama, "Did you hear what Grandpapa called me when he was lying on the ground?"

Anna searched her memory. She replayed the events in her mind: Christian had rushed up to Grandpapa and said, "Oh, Grandpapa, please don't die yet!" He had rubbed Grandpapa's cheek and stroked his hair. That seemed to help Grandpapa rouse a bit. Here Anna's memory paused.

After a bit her memory kicked in.

"Yes, I know what he called you!" Anna told him triumphantly.

"What was it?" Christian asked. Anna could tell he already knew the answer, but he wanted to hear her say it.

"He said, 'Christian, my young man.'" Anna was smiling as she looked at her son. "Christian, you have proven yourself to be a young man in the way you have watched over Grandpapa. You even wanted to carry his comforter. And right now when your papa is gone, you are taking his place as the man of the family."

Christian looked thoughtful. He had enjoyed being called a young man by Grandpapa, Anna knew. But it appeared to be a rather heavy responsibility for him to be the acting man of the family at nine years of age!

A light rain had started to fall, but now it picked up speed. Soon rain was coming in buckets. Anna could hear little Michel crying, and Katharina brought him back to his mama. In the pelting rain, Anna did her best to shield his little face. But the rain was soaking them all.

Barbara and Hans held onto Christian's hands, and Anna admired his ability to help them forward in the rain. Anna, herself, slipped and almost fell on mud and wet leaves.

The children were quite brave, and Barbara didn't complain about wet feet, but Anna knew that with her new style of open-toed shoes, rain must be saturating her toes.

The sound of hoof beats and squeaky cart wheels made Anna look up. Four carts were arriving again! This time Anna and her children were to get a ride as well as other parents with young children.

Christian picked up Barbara and put her in a cart and helped Hans up. Then he clambered up and reached out his hands to take little Michel. Last of all, Anna climbed in as well.

The rain had subsided, but Anna tried to imagine what a dripping wet bunch of emigrants they would be entering Mrs. Jakob Kohler's likely tidy house!

Little Michel seemed to enjoy his bumpy ride and imitated the sound of the squeaky wheels. Soon he had Christian, Hans, and Barbara laughing at his little antic. Anna smiled at her children's fun and found her tension easing with the humor they enjoyed.

As they drove up to the large Kohler home, Anna gazed in amazement at the copious dwelling with its massive third story overhang and balcony.

"Umm. . . no wonder Jakob Kohler felt free to invite us all to his home. Looks like there should be floor space for everyone!" Anna smiled in relief at the thought of a roof over their heads.

"And how are you, my dear one?" She turned as she heard her husband's voice. He was already lifting Barbara out of the cart. Then he took the baby while the boys hopped out. Last of all, he helped his wife to get down.

Mrs. Kohler introduced herself at the door, "Hello, I'm Jakob's wife, Elsbeth," said the diminutive lady, "and I want to welcome you all to our home." Her smile was like a sunbeam, and in spite of her petite size, there was nothing small about her generous heart or her hospitality for her sudden guests.

"Thank you so much, Mrs. Kohler," Anna exclaimed, "you don't know what it means to be welcomed, in our time of need, by kind people like yourselves! But we have been drenched by the rainstorm and I don't wish to make your home untidy," she said apologetically.

"My dear lady," Mrs. Kohler soothed, "our home is here for everyone who needs it. And what is a little dirt? I have daughters who clean my house."

In the large living area, Anna saw Grandpapa Michel, who, though appearing a little pale, looked as contented as a king in his castle.

Christian walked over and sat beside him, happy for the chance to be near his grandpapa again. "Christian, my young man," Grandpapa said, "I think you helped to revive me when I lay on the ground. I heard you say, 'please don't die yet'. And I felt you rubbing my check. Only then did I hear your papa talking to me. Later he told me he had talked to me when I couldn't respond. I'm feeling better now. These folks are taking good care of me, even giving me food to eat." Grandpapa was in high spirits again!

Elsbeth Kohler hovered over young Barbara, helping her to take off her wet shoes. "My little girl," Anna heard Elsbeth say, "Your shoes are open at the toes. No wonder your stockings are so wet!"

"Papa opened my shoes because they were too small and my feet hurt."

"So, you need bigger shoes," Elsbeth remarked sympathetically.

Barbara nodded.

"I think I can do something about that. You stay here and I will get a pair of shoes that may fit you quite well," Elsbeth told her.

When that generous lady returned, she not only had a pair of shoes for Barbara to try on, she also had a dry dress and stockings.

"I have girls who have outgrown these clothes, and I will be glad if you can wear them," Elsbeth explained to Barbara.

Barbara's eyes were sparkling as she picked up the shoes and clothes "Thank you," she said shyly to Mrs. Kohler.

"You are welcome. It's about time a little girl came along to fit these shoes and this dress."

Elsbeth led Anna to a room where she could change Barbara's clothes. Then Elsbeth said, "Just wait!" Soon she was back with a dress for Anna to wear. "This belongs to my daughter, Christina, but you need something dry to wear."

Elsbeth bustled about finding dry clothing for others as well.

Meanwhile, five of Jakob and Elsbeth's daughters scurried around the kitchen preparing venison and vegetable stew for the emigrants. The mingled aromas of freshly baked bread and savory stew wafted from the kitchen. Then pails of milk and plates of sliced apples appeared.

As the refugees sat around eating the delicious food they were served, Anna glanced at her family. What a blessing to have plenty of nourishing food for the little stomachs which had recently been aching from hunger!

It was almost too wonderful to be true! All unexpectedly God had blessed them with gracious hosts, warmth and protection of a safe home, food in abundance to satisfy even the heartiest of appetites, and a place to sleep in peace.

The Schenk children, tired from the traumatic events of the day, fell asleep almost immediately in the corner of a room assigned to them. Michel finally had a chance to talk privately with his wife. "I didn't want to leave you today, my dear one, but I didn't seem to have a choice. Papa needed me."

"Of course," whispered Anna, "you certainly did the right thing. And if Jakob and Daniel had not come along, where would we be?" She shuddered thinking of dear Grandpapa lying so helplessly on the ground.

"But tell me this, what gave you the confidence to go with Jakob?" Anna inquired softly.

Michel chuckled a bit, "I had to think fast to catch up with Jakob because he obviously had a plan of action which was meant to be followed! First of all, we were in a dire situation. How were we going to care for Grandpapa? Second, even if Jakob were meaning to turn us over to the authorities, he already knew where we were and we couldn't have gotten away quickly with my papa in that condition. Third, Anna, I sensed a peace from God about going with that man."

"Yes," whispered Anna, "they have done us only good. What a blessing from the Lord!"

– TEN –

Compassion

THE NEXT MORNING JAKOB TOLD THE men, "It appears that Michel Schenk needs rest and nourishing food for a few days. Your group is most welcome to stay until he is ready to travel again.

"My sons Isaak, Josef, and Samuel have taken their bows and arrows to hunt deer. We grew lots of vegetables, so food is plentiful here. And we are glad to host you as long as you wish to stay."

"Thank you from the bottom of our hearts for all your wonderful kindness, food, and lodging," Michel II replied, and other brothers chimed in with their thanks.

After breakfast, the Kohler home turned into a buzz of activity. Anna was grateful that Elsbeth had decided to wash clothes for the refugees. Anna and other ladies eagerly helped with the laundry. Many of them were wearing clothes borrowed from the Kohlers.

Anna poked her head into the kitchen to thank the

Kohler girls who were preparing food for later in the day.

She met the oldest daughter, Katharina, who seemed to be the head cook. Her younger sisters, Verena, Anna, Barbara, and Madlena were cutting vegetables for the soup while the venison and broth bubbled in the iron kettle.

The able-bodied brothers helped Jakob and his sons, Hans, Peter and Daniel, chop and stack wood.

Although the air was cool, the sun shone warm on the laundry spread out to dry. In one of her treks carrying laundry, Anna heard Jakob telling her husband, "Here is the opening to the Anabaptist escape tunnel, which leads to the woods where in the past Anabaptists could escape because it ends in a different jurisdiction from this one. The authorities pursuing them had no authority to arrest them in that jurisdiction."

"Anabaptist escape tunnel!" Anna's brain whirled. She didn't know such a thing existed. Even if the Kohlers weren't of this faith themselves, they certainly must be Anabaptist sympathizers, or half-Anabaptists, because they were aware that they were sheltering Swiss Brethren.

Christina and Margrith Kohler offered to play with the small children so their parents could be free to help with jobs. When Christina smiled, her face lit up like a sunbeam, and Margrith had an inviting way to make children feel at ease. Even little Michel warmed up to the girls.

Christian, Hans, Heinrich, and Niklaus helped stack wood. Anna could see them acting like little men as they hurried toward the wood pile with chunks almost too heavy for them to carry. One of the boys accidentally bumped Christian, knocking the heavy piece of firewood out of his arms and onto his foot. Anna saw Christian wince, but he said nothing. A bit later, she saw him limping slightly.

"Come sit here," Anna motioned to Christian. "Let me have a look at your foot." He winced again when she pulled off his shoe and sock. His foot was turning purple.

"That looks painful to me." Michel had slipped up behind Christian. "And it's swelling a little," he observed.

Christian's sorrowful eyes met his papa's steady gaze. "I – I wanted to help!"

"You were a wonderful helper, son," Michel said, "but now you'll need to have a little time off."

Elsbeth brought a cold, wet cloth and placed it on Christian's foot to bring down the swelling.

Niklaus rushed up to him, "Christian, I think I bumped you. Is that why the wood fell on your foot?"

Christian grinned a little. "That's all right, Niklaus. It should feel better soon."

It really did hurt, but Christian tried to think of something else. He loved to sing, so he distracted himself by singing the hymn his papa had led one morning:

"Rejoice, rejoice, ye Christians all, And break forth into singing!
Since far and wide on ev'ry side The Word of God is ringing.
And well ye know, no human foe Our souls from Christ can sever;

*For to the base and men of grace, God's Word
stands sure forever."*

His singing attracted the young children, who ran to
find out where it was coming from. Margrith and Christina had to run to catch up with them. Barbara and little
Michel plopped down beside Christian and joined him
in song. All of the little ones wanted to sing! Even with
some small voices off-key, it was a sweet, joyful noise.

Some of the men exchanged smiles as they worked,
and the women stopped for a few moments to enjoy the
young choir.

When Jakob discovered that the emigrants sometimes
had Scripture testimony, he said he would enjoy hearing
that after the evening meal.

It was dark outside when the group finally assembled
in the large living area before retiring to bed. Suddenly,
they heard a loud knock on the front door.

Jakob walked to the door and opened it. "Why, my
brother, Ludwig Kohler, what brings you here this evening?" he asked cheerfully.

"As constable in this jurisdiction, I've observed suspicious activity on your property and I've come to investigate," Ludwig said in a commanding voice.

"Of course, a constable is on duty day and night."
Jakob's congenial tone was matched by his agreeable
statement.

But Jakob immediately began a story before Ludwig
had a chance to speak. "I remember a little incident about

a man who was robbed and badly injured by thieves, and then he was left in a pitiful shape. A religious man came along and saw the unfortunate victim, but heartlessly left without helping him. Another religious man appeared on the scene, took a look at the ill-treated man, then mercilessly went his way. Then a second-class citizen came that way, saw the needy man, and with powerful compassion poured healing oil and wine into the man's wounds. He gave the victim a ride on his own animal for overnight lodging and paid the innkeeper to care for the injured one until he could return.

"Yesterday, I saw an ailing man, stretched out on the ground because of insufficient nourishment and overexertion. He, too, had been robbed. He had been robbed of proper food and of the comfort and rest of his own home. Why? Because his conscience told him to believe differently than the dictates of the state church.

"What do you think, brother? Do you think this guiltless man and his fellow travelers who are pushed from our land deserve compassion?" Jakob looked squarely at Ludwig.

Ludwig finally answered, "Compassion, yes. You are more honorable than I am because you have the love of God in your heart. So these folk are leaving the land?" His voice had lost its sternness.

"They certainly are. They have come from the Eggiwil area, but as you well know, it is a little distance to the border. Meanwhile, they need a place to receive nourishment and rest."

"I will do my best to protect you and your guests." With that Ludwig cordially bowed his head, acknowledging the refugees, and disappeared.

The atmosphere was so quiet it could be felt. Finally Jakob said it would be good if they saved the Scripture testimony for the next morning. He asked the elderly Christian Stauffer to lead in a prayer before they all retired for the night.

"Lord," Christian prayed, "we hallow Your name, and we praise You for You are worthy. We bless you for Your deliverance this night.

"We thank you for the great kindness of Jakob and his family. Bless them with Your guidance and Your peace.

"Please give us all rest this night.

"In the name of Jesus, our Saviour and Lord. Amen."

– ELEVEN –

A Strange Messenger?

COULD I HELP YOU IN THE KITCHEN TO-day?" Anna offered to the Kohler girls who were busily preparing food.

Katharina broke into a smile, "Yes, we would be glad for your help!"

The kitchen buzzed with work and conversation, and Anna thoroughly enjoyed preparing food again. But even more, she appreciated friendship with the Kohler girls. They were so wholesome in their outlook and so gracious about hosting the large group of emigrants. It seemed they enjoyed the fellowship, too.

When the emigrants and the Kohler family were eating, Jakob announced that Christian Stauffer was planning to give a Scripture testimony after the meal was finished.

The elderly brother began his testimony, "Brothers and sisters in Christ, only by the Lord's grace and mercy am I with you today. Never once has He failed me.

"My appointment as a minister among the Swiss Brethren was a serious responsibility for me. With the Lord's help, the Word of God was a treasure for me to unlock to feed the flock. I was concerned about each sheep in the flock. If faced with persecution, would each one be able to stand and be faithful? Who would hold the flock together if their leader were imprisoned? I thought of the Apostle Paul's statement in Acts, 'after my departing shall grievous wolves enter in among you, not sparing the flock'. But Christ gave me the assurance that He is Lord of the church and that I needed to rest in His power to guide and keep each one of the flock. I simply committed my brothers and sisters, my family, and myself to the Lord's keeping.

"One late night in 1644, when I was fast asleep dreaming of a beautiful Emmental spring morning—glimpsing placid goats and grazing cattle—a loud menacing knock startled me out of sleep. In my half-groggy state, I wanted to lie still and hope the person would go away.

"But when an angry voice yelled into the night, 'You minister, Christian Stauffer, come to the door, or we will break our way into the house!' I was stirred into quick action.

"Trembling, I pulled on my warmest clothing, rapidly giving my love and farewell to my wife, and went to face the *mouth of the lion* outside my door.

"My brothers in Christ, Uli Nüwhus and Uli Zaugg, had already been apprehended and were standing in the cold, bleak night with two constables.

"I had long envisioned that one day I would face arrest. But I had mentally pictured the time as early morning, just after leaving our night-time secret meeting. I would be fully cognizant, and Christ within me would guide my response. I had committed myself to walking in the footsteps of Jesus. During His trial, persecution, and crucifixion, He calmly and faultlessly faced the abuse heaped upon Himself.

"But the night of my arrest, I found myself confused and disoriented. Perhaps that was the purpose of a late-night arrest—to catch us bewildered.

"We were marched along with the smart-stepping constables. I shamed myself for not meeting my captors with the calmness that my Saviour had met His. With my coat sleeve, I wiped tears from my eyes.

"Suddenly, a stinging blow hit my cheek. 'He's weeping', one of the constables mocked. 'He's a leader of his people, and he can't take a little persecution'!"

"I saw the futility of trying to explain, so I remained quiet.

"The night engulfed us in darkness and misery. But then, the Lord Himself sent a reassuring promise, 'Lo, I am with you always, even unto the end of the world'.

"We walked on and on toward Thun Castle. But nothing mattered anymore. I was lost to the world, and the world was lost to me because I was in the presence of my Saviour and enjoying sweet communion.

"On that frigid trek from Eggiwil to Thun, I thought of my own experience and Jesus' requirement for His followers, 'If any man will come after me, let him deny himself, and take up his cross, and follow me. For whosoever will save his life shall lose it: and whosoever will lose his life for my sake shall find it. For what is a man profited, if he shall gain the whole world, and lose his own soul? Or what shall a man give in exchange for his soul? For the Son of man shall come in the glory of his Father with his angels; and then he shall reward every man according to his works'.

"I thought of some earlier Anabaptists who had lost their lives for their faith in Christ. Felix Manz had suffered drowning in Zurich's Limmat River, and Michael Sattler had bravely endured horrific pain until the flames ended his life.

"The morning sky was bright, but the air was very cold when we reached Thun Castle. The constables informed the prison authorities of our crime which was non-compliance with the state church.

"While we were escorted to our new lodging, my senses noted with precision the steps we took and the route to our cell.

"Uli Nüwhus and Uli Zaugg and I settled into our new home—that is, mentally and emotionally. We had no material possessions to unpack, as our only clothes were the ones we wore. Although we had put on our warmest garments, we still were not warm, as the temperature inside seemed as cold as it had been outside.

"We were fully awake, of course, when we arrived and emotionally keyed up. We decided to spend time praying and singing. We thanked the Lord for His great salvation, for His protection, and for His authority over all the earth. We interceded for our brothers and sisters, our wives, and our children. We ask for mercy on the constables and prison keepers.

"Then we sang until our voices gave out. One particularly special text was Michael Sattler's song, 'If One Ill Treat You for My Sake.'"

At this point Christian asked Michel II to lead the hymn. As she sang, Anna thought of her dear grandpapa Stauffer singing this meaningful hymn in a chill, bleak, prison cell:

> "If one ill treat you for My sake,
> And daily you to shame awake;
> Be joyful, your reward is nigh,
> Prepared for you in Heav'n on high.
> Fear not the man of such ill will;
> The body only can he kill;
> A faithful God the rather fear,
> Who can condemn to darkness drear.
> O Christ, help Thou Thy little flock,
> Who faithful follow Thee, their Rock;
> By Thine own death redeem each one,
> And crown the work that Thou hast done."

"That first day, we spent much of our time sleeping, as we were exhausted from our trek.

"Day after day our meals consisted of thin soup, bread,

and water. We were thankful for the sustenance. Day after day, we prayed and sang.

"One day we had a comforting surprise! Our wives had been informed where we were and sent comforters to the prison for us. We thanked God for this amazing solace!

Anna glanced around the circle of faces. Even the Kohlers were intently absorbed in Grandpapa's account.

"One night," he continued, "I was wrapped in my comforter. With this warmth I could sleep better than I had before. But then I was awakened by a slight movement wrapped in the comforter with me. I felt around and discovered I had a bed mate—a furry body with a long tail! As if being imprisoned were not enough infliction. Now that I was able to enjoy the solace of a comforter, why should I share that comfort with a mere mouse.

"I impulsively picked up the creature by the tail and hurled it toward the opposite wall. Thud! It slammed against the wall with a resounding smack!

"'Good'! I thought smugly. 'I think I've taken care of that pest'!"

"My gloating was short-lived when I discovered I had indeed killed my furry bed-fellow. Reality began to clear my foggy brain. A dead mouse is also a decomposing mouse. And in time, a decomposing mouse wafts out a putrid odor!

"But I was so tired I decided not to think about it for the time being and go back to sleep. Sleep, however, eluded me. I thought about the innocent mouse, which was seeking some comfort. I had considered it a pest.

"I realized I was a pest to the state church, because I would not subscribe to its teaching. Suppose the authorities had swiftly removed me as I had removed the mouse? I reflected on the mercy of my Heavenly Father.

"Then my brain further defogged. Suppose, just suppose, the mouse had been God's strange messenger sent to awaken me and nudge me to leave this prison? Shocking thoughts aroused my brain . . . suppose my brothers and I would try to escape? Suppose the prison doors would actually be unlocked!

"I whispered to them, 'Brothers, what do you think? Do you think possibly the Lord allowed that mouse to awaken me? Do you think God is providing unlocked doors for our escape'?

"'I dreamed this very night that we walked out of this castle', confessed Uli Zaugg. 'But still, is it safe to make an attempt? If we are caught, will something terrible befall us'?"

"We prayed together that we would discern the will of God and be united about any action we took.

"After we prayed, both of the brothers said they felt calmness from the Lord to try the doors.

"With a strange mixture of delirium and trust, I cautiously tried our cell door. We shouldn't have been surprised. But we were! It opened without a squeak, and we quietly inched our way through the doorway. I led the way as I remembered the route we had followed when we came into the castle. We had been led into a back entrance. Quietly we walked, praying as we went. Finally, we reached the exit door and cautiously I opened the door. We crept over the threshold into the chill air.

"Stealthily we moved away from the castle and the town of Thun, breathing easier the more distance we put between ourselves and our prison cell.

"Our plan was to head for Schwarzenburg, where Uli Zaugg's friend lived. Heading first to our homes seemed like a sure formula for another arrest.

"In retrospect, we contemplated what may have happened. Did the congenial prison keeper purposely leave doors unlocked? Did the Lord unlock the doors for our escape?

"For us, this experience was both exhilarating and humbling! We felt a kinship with the Apostle Peter who was led from prison by an angel. We saw no angel, but we definitely felt the presence of the Lord!"

– TWELVE –

Conscience, Commitment, Courage

*T*HE NEW DAY DAWNED BRIGHT, BUT cold. Frost had layered its white blanket on top of the grass and leaves and left the felled trees slippery with moisture. After morning milking and breakfast, Jakob decided this was a good time for Scripture testimony while the outside dried off.

Michel Schenk I had been asked if he would give another testimony, and he agreed to share again.

Anna could see that his strength and enthusiasm were returning. It was wonderful to see him looking rested, bright-eyed, and happy.

"Can you believe," asked Michel, who was almost as tall as his six-foot son, "that when I was fourteen years old, I was short and slightly built? I was very self-conscious about my small size.

"Whenever Abraham, a young fellow of the village,

would see me he would call me 'small rabbit' and challenge me to wrestle. I tried to ignore him, because I had no interest in wrestling or fighting him in any way. I was sure I had no chance to win!

"One day when I was fourteen, my mama sent me to the village to purchase salt for her. As soon as I made my purchase and stepped from the shop, I saw my scowling young enemy waiting for me.

"You can imagine how I felt. He grabbed me and tossed me to the ground. Gloating over me, he scoffed, 'Come on, small rabbit, you need to muscle up a little. Then we could have a real fight.'"

"For anyone looking on, I'm sure I made quite a spectacle, small rabbit that I was, as I rolled over and attempted to stand. For good measure, he gave me a sturdy kick with his foot.

"Just then, I heard a familiar voice call out, 'Young man, do you have an explanation for tossing my brother to the ground'?" There stood my older, muscular brother Christian. Warmth flooded my being, and I inwardly thanked Christian for coming to my defense.

"Christian didn't fool around. He catapulted Abraham to the ground, then said, 'This, young man, is what it feels like to suddenly be looking at the sky, with the back of your head slammed to the ground'.

"I stood as tall as I could, gloating over my brother's victory.

"'Come, Michel, let's go and let this young man think about how he should treat people'.

"I went home that afternoon, but for some reason, I didn't feel like telling my papa about the incident. I justified myself by thinking, 'I didn't even do anything. Christian took care of the bully for me'.

"Many years later, I attended a secret meeting of believers who felt that our established church did not fully follow Christ. As an infant, I had been baptized, by order of the state church. At the secret meeting I heard about adult baptism administered to a person who repented of his sin, choosing to follow Christ and join His Kingdom. Baptism was his testimony of his new life in Christ. The Scripture made it clear that only those who could understand and choose to follow Christ should receive baptism. 'He that believeth and is baptized shall be saved'.

"I kept attending the secret meetings of Anabaptists. I could see that these believers sought to live like Christ and focused much on the teachings from the Sermon on the Mount. One sermon centered around our response to our enemies. What 'hit me between the eyes' were these words, 'Ye have heard that it hath been said, An eye for an eye, and a tooth for a tooth: But I say unto you, That ye resist not evil, but whosoever shall smite thee on thy right cheek, turn to him the other also'.

"I realized that the spirit of retaliation toward my boyhood enemy was still within me, and I was powerless to overcome it on my own. I began to examine myself, and I found that my feelings and my selfish desires dominated my thinking. But another desire rose within me. More than anything, I wanted to live the beautiful Christ-like life. So, I asked Jesus to come into my heart and change me into His image by His Holy Spirit. I looked to the blood of Jesus for cleansing from my sin. Then I received adult baptism.

"But even before my baptism, I knew I needed to make some things right from my past life. I started out by visiting my brother, Christian, who is with us on our journey.

"'Christian', I began, 'do you remember the boy, Abraham, who bullied me in town many years ago? He threw me to the ground. And then you knocked him to the ground'.

"Christian searched his memory. 'Now that you mention it, yes, I believe I do'.

"'Do you think we should apologize to Abraham and ask his forgiveness'? I queried.

"'Certainly, that would be the Christlike thing to do', Christian agreed.

"We decided to look up Abraham that very day.

"It took us nearly two hours to walk to Signau where Abraham lived. We had lived there when we were young. We ask where Abraham lived and were directed to his home.

"His face no longer wore the countenance of a bully. His manner was friendly as we entered the chalet. 'Hello, Christian and Michel! I was thinking of you one day recently. How interesting that you should show up at my house today! I wanted to tell you, Michel, how sorry I was for the way I taunted you when you were young. I especially remember tossing you to the ground in a mean stunt. Will you forgive me'?"

"'Certainly, I will forgive you, Abraham," I told him.

"Then Christian spoke, 'I was wrong to retaliate and throw you on the ground. Will you forgive me'?"

"'I will forgive you from my heart', Abraham replied warmly. 'Christ has been merciful in leading me to salvation. And God gave me a wonderful wife and children, which I did not deserve. You see, I was a very troubled youth. My papa had died when I was five years old. Mama worked hard to keep our family together and to keep up the farm work, or prod her children into doing much of it.

"'Since I was the youngest of her six children, I had a little more leisure time than the others, and I would sneak off to town and torment boys like you. I was frustrated with my life, and this was a vent for my frustration.

"'Abraham, I had no idea how difficult your life was. I'm so sorry that most of your growing up years you had no papa. I'm also sorry for the mean thoughts I had toward you and that I was glad Christian tossed you down. Please forgive me. Now I'm a follower of Christ and I want His love to rule my life.'"

"Abraham forgave me and we parted as brothers in Christ.

"Not long after that we heard that Abraham had died. What a blessing it was for Christian and me to know that forgiveness had been extended all around."

Anna had observed her son Christian's response to his grandpapa's testimony. He seemed totally absorbed in his own world, as if only he and Grandpapa were in the room. "This trip is doing a lot to mature him," thought Anna. "He was pleased to be called young man. He is becoming one."

Jakob and Elsbeth and their youth seemed to value the fellowship of the refugees and listened with a sense of wonder during Scripture testimony time. The group of Anabaptists were amazed and overwhelmed with the hospitality the Kohler family showed them.

Anna found herself working in the kitchen with Katharina and Madlena Kohler plus Anabaptist ladies, Margareta Roet and Katharina Schneider.

Elsbeth Kohler and her daughters, Verena, Anna, and Barbara, and a few refugee ladies cleaned and tidied the large house and mended clothing for the Anabaptist ladies.

Christina was overjoyed to entertain and care for the young children again. The little ones sat wide-eyed as Christina vividly described scenes from the Bible. The children sang lustily under Margrith's capable direction. Once she asked Anna's son, Christian, to come and teach them new songs.

Jakob and his crew of men chopped nearly all of the felled trees and carried the larger pieces, while young boys took the smaller chunks to the woodpile.

While Anna cleaned and cut a large pile of carrots, she visited with the Kohler girls.

"With our large family we need a lot of vegetables," explained Madlena, "so we always grow plenty. Since our garden produced well this year, we have more than usual."

"The kindness of your family has overwhelmed us!" Anna told her.

"We have enjoyed your people so much." Katharina chimed in. "It has been a blessing to see how peaceful your elderly as well as your young families are in the midst of the difficult circumstances you have been through. My family feels you should be allowed to stay in Canton Bern and serve the Lord the way you feel is right. How can you so calmly accept your exile from this land?"

"Katharina, we have accepted the fact that we needed to leave, since our consciences were not in agreement with the state church creeds. We are committed to following Christ and his teachings, and He gives us the courage to take the steps we do day by day. These words from Jesus are very precious to me, 'Peace I leave with you, my peace I give unto you: not as the world giveth, give I unto you. Let not your heart be troubled, neither let it be afraid'.

"But I will admit, I have struggled with fears. However, I am learning to trust Christ more than I ever did before. I may not have an easy life, but Christ has promised, 'I will never leave thee, nor forsake thee.'"

Katharina looked as if she were pondering what Anna said. "Anna, you have such a sincere trust in Christ. I wish…"

Anna spoke softly. "Your family's care for us has shown us how God provided for us in our time of dire need. Thank you from the bottom of my heart."

The kitchen buzzed with meal preparation. Venison and broth bubbled slowly in the iron kettle. Anna finished up the carrots and carefully dropped them into the broth. Someone else added potatoes.

The tantalizing smell of freshly baked bread filled the air. Crisp apples whetted the appetites of those who had been hard at work.

Soon their group of emigrants would need to leave, Anna knew. But the warm-hearted fellowship, nourishing food, and roof provided over their heads were like a gift sent down from heaven!

– THIRTEEN –

Sow in Tears, Reap in Joy

AT BREAKFAST THE NEXT MORNING, Michel Schenk I told the Kohler family, "How can I thank you enough for your excellent care of me these past days? I believe the Lord used your family to help save my life! 'The Lord bless thee, and keep thee: The Lord make his face shine upon thee, and be gracious unto thee: The Lord lift up his countenance upon thee, and give thee peace.'"

What he said next left a sigh of regret hanging in the air. The Kohlers had felt a deepening friendship with the emigrants. And the thought of their departure put a damper on the atmosphere as Michel said, "I have recovered so well that I feel ready to start out again tomorrow morning."

"We cannot hold you here," Jakob finally said, "but your group has taught us what it means to trust the Lord in the midst of difficulty. We know we can also learn other valuable lessons from you. So today we will sit together and have your brothers guide us through teachings of Scripture."

A knock sounded loudly on the door. When Jakob opened it, there stood his brother, Ludwig.

"My son and I need to pick up supplies in the village today, and both of our carts need to be fixed. Might we borrow two of your carts?"

"Certainly, Ludwig and Georg, but if you have a bit of time you may want to listen to an Anabaptist brother give a Scripture testimony first.

Ludwig hesitated, and then concluded, "Ye-s, since we don't need to go until this afternoon, maybe we could stay here a little longer."

Georg threw his papa a puzzled look.

But Ludwig stepped into the house, followed by a hesitant Georg.

Hans and Katharina Schneider were a young Anabaptist couple near the ages of Michel II and Anna Schenk. Katharina was a picture of grace as she gathered her son and two small daughters close to her, while her husband, Hans, stood up to give the Scripture testimony.

"I wonder how the God of heaven felt when He watched his Son, Jesus, suffer under the piercing crown of thorns. How He must have grieved when He saw Jesus receiving the mockery of a scarlet robe and a reed in His hand. What pangs did He feel when He saw His Son spit upon and struck with a reed? And did the excruciating pain of the crucifixion of His Son pierce His Father heart?

"Jesus Himself taught us that death comes before life, when He said, 'The hour is come, that the Son of man should be glorified. Verily, verily, I say unto you, Except a corn of wheat fall into the ground and die, it abideth alone: but if it die, it bringeth forth much fruit',

"The God of heaven orchestrated the bright day of resurrection after the dark day of crucifixion. The death and resurrection of Christ were essential to our own spiritual birth.

"In March 1670, my wife and I became parents of a dearly beloved son, whom we named Hans. He grew and developed as a baby should. But when he was one year old, he became sick with fever. We asked the Lord, if it was His will, to heal our small son. We tried every remedy we knew. And we asked aid from the village lady who had helped many sick children to recover health. His fever, however, became worse. My wife and I held his little body as we continued to place cold cloths on his hot little forehead. His eyes fluttered open only occasionally. Our hearts were torn with grief as his little body weakened. So, this was what it was like to watch one's own precious baby die?

"We sat and held him together as we watched him breathe more and more slowly. We told him over and over that we loved him, but that he could go to be with Jesus now. Finally, we saw him take his last breath.

"In those moments of sorrow and reality, we found ourselves pleading, 'God, please stay with us'.

"Our little son had passed from this life late at night.

On into the night Katharina and I felt the fresh, raw pangs of grief, as we continued to hold his little body."

Tears rolled down Katharina's cheeks as she listened to her husband recount their story. Ludwig put his head in his hands. Many of the women sat sympathetically crying.

"In our grief, we also experienced a measure of God's grace, as we claimed this Scripture, 'Thou wilt keep him in perfect peace, whose mind is stayed on thee: because he trusteth in in thee'."

"We had not had this son baptized as required by the state Reformed church, because of our conviction from Scripture that 'he that believeth and is baptized shall be saved'. We knew infants were too young to understand belief in Christ. We felt that our innocent son was now at rest, tenderly cared for in the heavenly realm.

"Much as I wanted to sit with my wife, I suddenly realized, with a sense of urgency, my new responsibility. Since our son had not been baptized, we could not consider burying his little body in the Reformed church graveyard. I knew that before daylight, it would be wise to dig the small grave in a secluded spot and frame together a wooden box in which to bury his little body. In the slim moonlight, I finally completed the grave.

"Around three o'clock in the morning, Katharina and I gently woke our six-year-old son David, and three-year-old twin daughters, Maria and Susanna, and told them their baby brother, Hans, had gone to be with Jesus. We let them each hold their little brother's body. Then we carefully placed it in the little box. Together we walked

The beautiful snow-terraced Hohgant, an Emmental Alps mountain, can be seen from near the Knubel area of Eggiwil, Switzerland.

The historic Swiss Reformed church building in Eggiwil, Switzerland, where Michel Schenk II and Anna Stauffer were married on September 21, 1660. Their son, Christian Stauffer Schenk, was christened here in 1662.

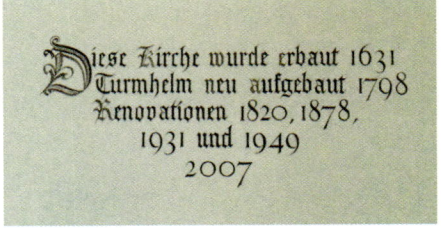

Diese Kirche wurde erbaut 1631
Turmhelm neu aufgebaut 1798
Renovationen 1820, 1878,
1931 und 1949
2007

Translated into English, a plaque in the church building reads as follows: This church was built in 1631; Spire rebuilt in 1798; Renovations in 1820, 1878, 1931 and 1949, 2007.

An interior view of the church building shows the chancel in the front and a section of the pulpit with its sounding board, to the extreme right.

This spacious home in the Sumiswald area of Switzerland is mentioned in the story as the dwelling of the fictitious Jakob Kohler family who hosted the Eggiwil Swiss Brethren.

An Anabaptist escape tunnel lay beneath
the historic Sumiswald home pictured on the
opposite page. From this tunnel Anabaptists
could escape to a forest where Anabaptist
hunters were not allowed to hunt for them as it
was beyond their jurisdiction. At a later time,
however, this restriction on the Anabaptist
hunters no longer applied.

Hinten, Eggiwil, Switzerland, was the birthplace of Michel Schenk II in 1639. This historic looking house nestles into the sloping landscape in the Hinten area.

Perhaps the Schenks enjoyed pastoral views of scenic Swiss hillsides such as the one pictured here.

Swiss cows, Emmentaler cheese, and the Swiss countryside are all part of the essence of this lovely land.

to the grave site.

"I recited these words from I Corinthians, 'So also is the resurrection of the dead. It is sown in corruption; it is raised in incorruption: It is sown in dishonour; it is raised in glory: it is sown in weakness; it is raised in power. It is sown a natural body; it is raised a spiritual body'. I commit the precious little body of Hans Schneider to this earth to be one day raised in glory. Praise God for this resurrection to come. Our farewell, dear Hans, until we meet again.

"Our parents and a number of other people had known Hans was sick. When they found out he had died, we were visited and supported with sympathy, prayers, food, and helpfulness. The Reformed minister visited us in a kindly manner.

"But my wife and I were unprepared for the harshness that followed.

"'I want you to know', one lady told us, 'if you had allowed your baby to be baptized, he would not have died! I hope you learned your lesson. You can't defy the law of God and get by'!

"A man and wife from the village stopped by.

"He announced, 'See what happened because your son was not baptized! It doesn't pay to disobey the law of the land. What authority do you have to decide what the Scripture says about baptism? Only the leaders of the state church can decide that'!

"In spite of our emotional pain, we knew the Christ-like response was to show kindness. So, we thanked them for coming.

"We were comforted by this Scripture, 'These things have I spoken unto you, that in me ye might have peace. In the world ye shall have tribulation; but be of good cheer; I have overcome the world.'" With that, Hans took his seat.

"Our dear Brother Hans and Sister Katharina," said Michel II, "we love you and we suffer with you today for the pain you still feel over the loss of your little Hans. May the God of grace simply surround you with His comfort."

Other brothers and sisters also expressed love and sympathy. A tear ran down Ludwig's cheek, and even Georg's eyes were watery, but those two men said nothing.

Hans Schneider spoke up again, "Just as for our Lord Jesus, a day of triumph, the resurrection, came after one of seeming tragedy, the crucifixion, so, the sorrow of our little one's death ends in the triumph of his destiny. Praise God, Katharina and I expect to see him some day."

"Further, in my mind's eye, I see a new day dawning for those who wish to follow Christ according to their consciences and their understanding of the Word of God. We are exiled from this land to journey to a land of relative religious freedom. But the sacrifices we make in our day, the possessions we leave behind, the sad farewell we bid to the land of our birth, are but small dust in our hands in contrast to the heritage we gain in Christ. What we 'sow in tears', so our children and many generations to come may 'reap in joy'. I believe, with Michel Schenk II, that our journey is a journey of destiny."

Anna saw a faraway look come into Jakob's eyes. Even Ludwig had lost his constable countenance.

Jakob said that everyone could walk out into the fresh air a bit and then assemble for a time of instruction from the Anabaptist brothers.

Anna hastened to talk with Elsbeth and Katharina Kohler. "Some of our Anabaptist ladies can take over meal preparation if you would like to listen to the discussion.

"If you really want to . . ." Elsbeth began.

"Sure, I would be glad to do that!"

Anna asked a number of ladies if they would like to help, and off they headed to the kitchen. Katharina Kohler also came to give a bit of direction about the meal.

As they quietly worked, Anna could hear some of the discussion taking place in the living area.

"If the state would allow each person to serve Christ according to his conscience, that would certainly be a peaceful and fair way to resolve this conflict." Anna heard Jakob remark. "Of course," he chuckled, "Anabaptism already has a lot of followers, but if freedom of religion were granted, many more people might leave the state church. So that would diminish church funds, which would not be a welcome thought for church authorities!"

"Yes, we certainly believe that in matters of faith, the church and state should be separate," commented Christian Schenk, "but of course the authorities never took our opinion on that matter," he chuckled.

Jakob spoke again, "I never understood what was so important about an adult baptism to the Anabaptists. But when Hans Schneider spoke about believing and being baptized, it made perfect sense."

"You wanted to know about swearing?" she heard someone say. "Matthew 5 has a section of verses which gives Jesus' teaching on the subject.

"'Swear not at all,' He said.

"And He went on to explain why we are not to swear. A simple 'yes' or 'no' is enough."

"How will our homeland be protected if our citizens do not rise up to defend this land and its people?" Jakob wondered.

Michel I spoke up, "You have asked a very good question, Jakob. This land is dear to our hearts. Tearing ourselves away is painful. But we have a higher loyalty, which is our loyalty to the Kingdom of God.

"Our king instructs us, 'resist not evil: whosoever shall smite thee on thy right cheek, turn to him the other also'.

"He further instructs us to love our enemies, and do good to them that hate us. If our believing young men should take sword in hand to kill our enemies, how could we reconcile such action with Christ's teaching? We respect the laws of the state and uphold them when they do not violate God's higher law. But defending our land is not the way of God's kingdom, but the kingdom of this world."

Jakob nodded his head, but seemed to be struggling to process all the novel teachings he was hearing. The Kohler young men also seemed to be deep in thought.

"Forgiveness is a major issue with Christ, because He made our forgiveness from God conditional on our willingness to forgive those who sin against us," the elderly

Christian Schenk remarked. "I knew a man who cheated me out of a lot of money. I struggled much with forgiveness. But one day as I read Matthew 6, these words stood out to me, 'And forgive us our debts, as we forgive our debtors'. I asked the Lord over and over to help me forgive that man. I have forgiven him many times, because many times I think of how he wronged me. I now have peace and forgiveness in my heart."

When the meeting ended, Ludwig and Georg rose to go.

The Anabaptist brothers, one by one, went to meet them and bid them farewell.

"I'm certainly glad to meet you!" Michel I remarked to Ludwig. "You must have the same tendency for mercy as does your brother, Jakob. May God return to you the same measure of kindness you have given to us."

– FOURTEEN –

Anabaptist Hunter

TRUE TO HIS DECISIVE AND HELPFUL nature, Jakob had a plan of action ready for the departure of the emigrants. His four horse-drawn carts would be used in transporting the most elderly Anabaptists.

After many thanks and farewells to the Kohler family, the Swiss Brethren started before dawn on their journey toward Biberist. Daniel, Isaak, Josef, and Samuel Kohler each drove a cart. Tucked into the corners of the carts were packets of food for everyone on the trip.

Jakob and two of his sons, Peter and Hans, walked with the rest of the Anabaptists and planned to meet up with those in the carts at certain spots along the route. This was familiar territory to Jakob, so he told his cart-driving sons where to make their first stop for those following on foot.

Gentle had soon adjusted to her routine of grazing in the pasture and bedding down in the barn with the Kohler cattle. Feasting on hay from the field, calmly chewing her cud, and munching grass with the other cattle had a tranquil effect on Gentle. With less stress and adequate food, she was giving more milk. So, when Ulrich Eymann led Gentle out of the comfortable barn on the early morning of their departure, she protested with bawling and a bit of hoof-dragging.

Jakob told the emigrants he had a friend, Heinrich Martin, below Biberist, where he planned to stop. Perhaps the Martins would be glad to offer overnight lodging to the Swiss Brethren.

As they started their early morning trek, Anna realized that their refreshing stop at the Kohlers had given them zest for this new leg of the journey. Little Michel, Barbara, Hans, and even Christian had enjoyed running, playing, and singing with the young Schneider and Roet children. The Kohlers' nutritious food had strengthened their bodies.

Barbara was happy that her shoes were large enough for her feet and stitched at the toes! She was now wearing the dress Elsbeth Kohler had given her to put on when they arrived. Elsbeth told Anna she could keep it, and since it was in better shape than Barbara's original dress, they left the old one behind.

As they walked along, Christian and Hans reminisced with Heinrich and Niklaus Roet about their fun times together stacking wood, running races, listening to Christina's Bible story-telling, and singing with Margrith.

Anna's mind went again and again to the blessing the

Kohler family had been to them all. She hoped she had thanked them adequately! Her prayer of gratitude ascended to the Lord for using this family to benefit them so abundantly.

With the most elderly riding ahead in carts, those on foot could move more quickly than usual. It was a good thing, too, because they needed rapid exercise to get their blood stirring quickly on this cold morning!

At last they reached the spot where the carts had stopped. Beautiful bands of rose and mauve colored the horizon. "God has a breathtaking palette for the morning sky," mused Anna.

As the pedestrians arrived at the meeting spot, they could hear the elderly singing a song of praise to God. The cold morning did not dampen their joy as they rubbed their hands together and pulled comforters around themselves.

Some of the men fetched drinking water from the Emme River, but the water was so cold Barbara and little Michel shivered and could not drink much.

"We are making good time," Jakob observed. "We should arrive at the Martin's while it is still daylight."

Abruptly, a menacing voice snarled, "Halt!" Before Anna could even find where the voice came from, she saw a sword flash through the air.

Michel II immediately threw his arms around his wife and children. Little Michel screamed, Hans's and Barbara's eyes grew wide, Christian turned white, and Anna's heart thumped wildly. There they stood, a huddled, defenseless family.

Christian Stauffer, Michel I, and others of the elderly bowed their heads, waiting for the blow to strike.

Jakob, as usual, took command of the situation. "Why," he asked authoritatively, "do we have such a disturbance?"

"Disturbance!" the sword-wielding man spat. "You heretic Anabaptists are causing the disturbance! You will not obey the state church! So, it's off to the prison in Bern for every one of you. Don't think because you are old you will be set free!" he shouted looking at Anna's Grand-papa Stauffer.

Anna had never seen such an evil looking man in all her life. His diabolical countenance was so unapproachable she could hardly look at him. It was then Anna noticed his companion in the background. He had not unsheathed his sword, and his face wore a sad expression.

"Did you realize, sir," Jakob pressed upon the Anabaptist hunter, "that with your unwarranted pronouncement, you could possibly receive a stiff punishment for your ill-behavior toward a group of people who are leaving this land? The state church minister in their village witnessed their departure from their area. It may not go well with you," Jakob said decisively.

"So, you are not one of them?" the Anabaptist hunter snarled at Jakob. "Why are you here? Don't you know that by helping these dogs you could pay a huge fine? I think it's time to report you to the authorities!" he sneered.

"Since my brother, Ludwig Kohler, is a constable, why don't we go see him together?" Jakob offered.

At that, the Anabaptist hunter spurred his horse and took off in anger. His companion meekly turned his horse and followed.

After he was well out of earshot, Jakob kindly explained, "No doubt, the Anabaptist hunter was looking forward to a huge bounty in reward money for catching this large group of Anabaptists."

Then Jakob spoke softly, "Why don't we thank God for sparing us from the sword?"

A murmur of assent rose up from the group. Many were well aware that, warranted or not, this agitated man could have unleashed fury with his sword on these defenseless believers.

Jakob asked Hans Schneider if he would lead in a prayer of gratitude for God's protection.

"Lord," Hans prayed, "thank you for the safety you gave us this very hour. Thank you for Jakob who has stood by us in our times of need. If we ever must give our lives for the sake of Christ, as many of our fellow believers in the faith have done, please give us grace to meet that summons. In the name of Jesus Christ, Amen."

Everyone quietly waited. Even Jakob looked a little pale. The emotional trauma had drained the group of its vigor for the time being.

Soon someone started singing the text that martyr Michael Sattler had penned many years before:

"If one ill treat you for My sake, And daily you to shame awake;
Be joyful, your reward is nigh, Prepared for you in Heav'n on high.
Fear not the man of such ill will; The body only can he kill;
A faithful God the rather fear, Who can condemn to darkness drear.
O Christ, help Thou Thy little flock, Who faithful follow Thee, their Rock;
By Thine own death redeem each one, And crown the work that thou hast done."

Singing seemed to bring rest to their spirits. They sang another song and another.

Suddenly they became aware that they were being observed. Michel glanced at Anna, and they exchanged smiles. For the countenances on the faces of the men who had stopped their horses and were listening were such a contrast to the face of the Anabaptist hunter who had just left that they were simply overwhelmed with relief!

– FIFTEEN –

God's Protection and Jakob's Care

$\mathcal{A}$N AWKWARD SILENCE REIGNED for a few moments. Then one of the young men on horseback spoke up. "I am Rudolph, and this is my brother, Josef Lehmann. I hope you don't mind . . . but we enjoyed your singing," he concluded.

"No, we don't mind," ventured Michel II. "It's wonderful to see friendly faces." He smiled broadly at the young men.

"And where are you from?" Josef asked.

"We are from the area of Eggiwil," Michel answered simply.

"We are from near Biberist, but my brother and I are on an errand to Burgdorf," Josef explained.

Unasked questions hung in the air. Finally, Rudolph decided to divulge more information. "We are Anabaptists, but we have not been hounded the way some of our fellow Anabaptists have been. We have only three families that meet and worship together."

"We are Anabaptists, too. We are leaving this land now to escape the threat of persecution. On our trek north, my papa was overcome with weakness and fainted. Jakob Kohler," he pointed out Jakob with a wave of his hand, "kindly came to our rescue, as an Anabaptist sympathizer, and even hosted us for a few days while Papa recovered. His six sons are with us, too."

"Are you fellowshipping with the Heinrich Martin family?" Jakob wanted to know.

"We certainly are," Josef responded, "and the Benedict Frei family."

Jakob continued, "I know Heinrich, and I thought perhaps these Anabaptist friends could have overnight lodging with his family."

"I think they would be glad to host you," Rudolph responded. "But since none of us have large houses, some of your group could come to the two other homes, as well."

Rudolph added as an aside, "We should be back from Burgdorf before long."

"It certainly was a relief to see your Christian countenances a while ago," commented Hans Roet. "Shortly before you arrived, we had a visitor of an opposite nature. He flashed a sword, if that tells you anything."

Jakob commented, "This large group of Anabaptists could have perhaps yielded bountiful reward money for the Anabaptist hunter." Then Jakob looked around the group, "But my friends, the Anabaptists, have a far greater treasure with their faith in Christ than this lamentable soul could ever have with a trove of money."

Michel and Anna smiled at each other. The more they learned to know Jakob, the more they appreciated him.

Michel II collected his young family for another leg of the trip. The carts started off, and Jakob led the pedestrians. At first, the children enjoyed crunching through fallen leaves. But before long that grew tiresome for the little feet that had lately been romping in the Kohlers' expansive yard. Little Michel grew tired of being carried. "Papa, down, down," he would say. Michel II would put him down to take a few steps, then scoop him up again.

Soon they met up with the carts again and ate from the provisions the Kohlers had sent. Even the adults felt an extra spurt of energy after that, and Jakob assured them it should not take more than two more hours to reach the Martin home.

Finally, Jakob led them into a clearing. A distance away, in the woods, the carts had waited for them. When Jakob saw that Heinrich was outside splitting wood, he walked up to his friend.

"Why Jakob Kohler!" exclaimed Heinrich, "What a pleasant surprise! We just heard you were on the way with a group of Anabaptists."

Heinrich's wife appeared in the doorway. "Hello, I'm Catri," she said beaming at them. "I want to welcome you here! We rarely get guests, and this will be a pleasure to host you. Rudolph and Josef Lehmann were eager to tell us all that special guests were on the way. You should have seen—their horses were sweating and panting from their run back from Burgdorf! Those boys!" she said with a twinkle in her eye and a broad smile on her face.

"If this is agreeable with your people," Heinrich said, "we will host your group in our three different homes."

"Of course," Michel II said, "It is very kind of your three families to lodge us for the night, and however you plan it will be fine!"

Catri and her three daughters were preparing a delicious meal of cooked venison and vegetables, which her husband persuaded Jakob and his sons to eat as well.

After the meal, Jakob quickly rallied his sons to start for their home. But before they slipped away, he told the Eggiwil brethren, "You have shown me the way of Christ. I want to follow that way."

Many of the brethren gave him encouraging words and told him they would pray for him and his family. Michel Schenk I gratefully said, "I feel you not only helped to save my life by taking me to your home. But it seems twice the Lord powerfully used you to avert persecution for us. Praise to God and much blessing to you, Jakob!"

With tears in their eyes and gratitude in their hearts, the brothers and sisters from Eggiwil waved off Jakob and his sons.

– SIXTEEN –

Christ Is Our Life

OON THE TWO OTHER HOST FAMI-
lies, the Bernhard Lehmann and the Benedict
Frei families met at Heinrich Martin's home
where they all shared out the guests who had arrived.

The Schenk's and others stayed at the Martin's for overnight. Exhausted, the emigrants bedded down early.

As usual, Michel and Anna woke before dawn—to
hear cows bawling for their morning hay. "No doubt Gentle is joining the cow chorus," thought Anna drowsily, as
she drifted into a dreamy stupor. When Michel and Anna
awoke again, the sun was peeping over the horizon.

"Such sleepy heads!" Michel observed.

"I know," Anna agreed, "I'm a bit ashamed we weren't
up sooner. We need to get into the routine of walking
again. Yesterday was pretty exhausting."

"That brush with the Anabaptist hunter drained our
emotions!" Michel said emphatically.

When everyone appeared for breakfast, Anna glanced around, hoping to meet the children of their host family. This was a younger family than the Kohler's, with three daughters sandwiched in between four sons. Georg was eighteen, Niklaus sixteen, Susanna fourteen, Elsbeth thirteen, Maria ten, Hans was eight and Stephan six.

Christian and Hans Schenk were delighted to make friends with the two young Martin boys near their ages.

"What do you like best about this trip?" Anna overheard Hans Martin asking her son Christian.

"The best part was being at Jakob Kohler's! We could run and play, stack wood, and, oh yes, have lots of food! But I like it here," he hastened to add, "You have lots of good food, too! And being with you boys is really great! Being here is much better than walking, walking, walking. I had forgotten how boring it was until some of us had to walk again yesterday."

The Lehmann's and the Frei's and their guests arrived, and everyone met in the living room.

Heinrich Martin stood up to speak and addressed the crowd for the Lord's Day service.

"It is with great pleasure that I welcome you all to this worship service today. I did not doubt that God was working among many believers here in our own land. But that was confirmed to me yesterday in the arrival of our fellow Christian believers from Eggiwil. To the believers from Eggiwil, I cannot begin to tell you what your faith and willingness to suffer have meant to me since your arrival yesterday. Jesus speaks about this sacrifice in Mark 10.

"Then Peter began to say unto him, "Lo, we have left all, and have followed thee'. And Jesus answered and said, 'Verily I say unto you, There is no man that hath left house, or brethren, or sisters, or father, or mother, or wife, or children, or lands, for my sake, and the gospel's, But he shall receive an hundredfold now in this time, houses, and brethren, and sisters, and mothers, and children, and lands, with persecutions; and in the world to come eternal life'.

"Many of you have felt the pain of separation from close family members—husband or wife left behind; children, grandchildren, or parents left behind—because you have chosen to follow Christ.

"My heart aches for you, and my prayers ascend for you. But even in the midst of your separation, your sorrow, and your suffering—there's hope! In God's Kingdom, our three families are your brothers and sisters, our houses and our lands are yours as long as you care to stay. Love and compassion flows from our hearts to your hearts. But the true reward awaits in the world to come, for it is eternal life!

"Now I want to encourage you with the message of Christ—Christ is our Life! Heinrich went on to describe how we can have life because Christ purchased our redemption through His death and the shedding of His precious blood. And he explained Christ's resurrection as the cornerstone of our faith.

"For those of you who feel the pain of family disruption, remember that Christ bought you to be part of His family. He is always ready to hear your prayer and to fellowship with you. And in the Christian family, you have many brothers and sisters.

When Heinrich sat down, Ulrich Stauffer was the first to thank Christ for the immeasurable gifts of redemption and resurrection. He also thanked Heinrich for his great encouragement. He said, "Among our emigrant families, probably everyone left behind some family member or another. My wife chose to stay in Eggiwil with our six children. This was the hardest thing I have ever had to face," Ulrich said softly. "My wife and I and our children loved each other and did not want to part, but they feared the many possible dangers of this journey. I prayed and pondered long and hard before I took this step, but I knew that I needed to leave the land in order to follow Christ honestly. In the midst of my pain, He has given me peace," Ulrich finished with tears trickling down his cheeks.

Hans Eymann and Niclaes Heiler shared similar experiences of leaving wives and children behind. Hans Jurien and his wife had brought only one of their three children along. But they, too, appreciated the encouragement of Christ's conquest over death.

The Martin, Lehmann, and Frei ladies provided a delicious lunch for everyone, and as Anna helped clean up afterward, she had an opportunity to talk with one of the emigrant ladies, Magdalena Kropf. Magdalena was a widow and none of her three children had come with her on the journey.

"Magdalena," Anna questioned gently, "did the talk

of missing family members open up a tender spot in your heart?"

"Yes, it did," Magdalena faced Anna with tears in her eyes, "but when that tenderness is brought out into the light, it has a much better chance of healing than when it's pushed far down into a dark and secret spot in my heart. The victory that we have in Christ encourages me to be faithful to Him regardless of missing family. Also, I'm comforted by fellowship with brothers and sisters, like yourself, who are my spiritual family. I can say truly, 'Christ is my life', and all believers in Christ are my family."

A JOURNEY OF DESTINY

– SEVENTEEN –

Plenty of Food

GOD IS TAKING GOOD CARE OF US! How blessed we have been sleeping in warm houses these last number of nights! But even in the hardships, God is always with us," Michel observed sagely to Anna when they woke up at the Martin's again the next morning.

"I know, and I sense His love, even in the difficult times. But He gives us enough comforts along the way to make the journey quite a bit easier," Anna replied.

"We will just face each day knowing that the Lord is in control," Michel continued soberly.

"I never dreamed we would have a family like the Kohler's helping us. And now it's the Martin's, Lehmann's, and Frei's! God simply saw our need and provided. It's humbling," Anna said softly.

"They really seem to enjoy having our people visit, and we enjoy them and their hospitality. Of course, their 'good food', as Christian mentioned, was most welcome!"

"So, you heard Christian talking with Hans Martin?" Anna laughed quietly.

"Yes, he was quite honest," admitted Michel. "But then, what healthy person doesn't like good food? Especially after eating skimpily!"

"Christian is such a people person, and I'm glad he can have good friends here," Anna added.

After breakfast, it was soon time for all the emigrants to gather at the Martin's and begin their day's trek toward Basel. Here, two of the scouts planned to search out a ship to take the Anabaptists down the Rhine River toward the Palatinate.

"Thank you for all your kindness," Michel II told the Martin's. "We are overwhelmed with your generosity and hospitality, including the good food!"

"Heinrich, Anna and I were blessed with your message yesterday. Focusing on Christ's redemptive work was a balm for us in our uncertain journey," Michel said.

Just then a child outside screamed! To Michel II it sounded like little Michel's voice.

He rushed out to find Christian and some other young boys loitering in the fresh air. Michel III, trembling and terrified, was clinging onto Christian. Christian and Hans, along with Hans and Stephan Martin, all wore blanched faces. Michel II quickly glanced about. At the edge of the clearing, the diabolical-looking Anabaptist hunter sat on his horse, menacingly brandishing his sword.

Wearing an appearance of bravery, Michel II took a

few steps forward. "Sir, is there something we could help you with? Perhaps a warm breakfast?"

Michel studied his face. He thought he saw a change in the man's countenance.

Michel continued, "You are most welcome—the food is plentiful!"

The man hung his head and tucked his sword back in its sheath. "I guess," he said gruffly, "if you want to bring it to me."

"Of course," Michel said evenly, but inwardly he breathed a huge sigh of relief. "I'll be back shortly."

He slipped into the kitchen where the ladies waited nervously and asked Anna to fetch a large bowl. He would explain later, he told her. Finding the pot of warm mixed grains, he filled the bowl and topped it off with fresh milk. "For our 'friend' the Anabaptist hunter'!" he whispered carefully.

But the ladies saw what was happening and prayed earnestly!

Michel hoped the man would not notice a slight tremor in his hands as he handed him the bowl. Michel flashed him a broad smile, "There's plenty more, so I'll be glad to refill your bowl when you are finished."

The Anabaptist hunter muttered, "Thank you," and set to work eating warm grains as if he were starved.

Michel distracted the young boys and led them behind the house, so they wouldn't gawk at the man on horseback.

"It would be good to stay here or go inside by the back

door," he instructed the boys.

When Michel reappeared in the clearing, the man had finished his grains. "Let me fill your bowl," he offered. Michel returned to the kitchen with the empty bowl, this time grinning to the ladies inside. Another large serving made its way outside, but this time Michel's hands did not tremble. He handed the bowl to the man, saying, "There's still more inside!"

"It tastes good," came the man's husky response.

Michel wandered about a bit, noticing that Heinrich and some of the men were stacking wood not far away where they could keep an eye on the happenings.

When Michel saw that the man had finished eating, he walked over and retrieved the bowl. "I'll bring you more," he stated matter-of-factly.

When the third helping was finished, Michel offered that the man could stay and visit with him.

But the well-fed man shook his head, and with a sad countenance, turned his horse and headed off.

Heinrich broke the silence that had reigned for a few minutes after he left, "Heaping coals of fire—or serving warm grains and milk—seems to have its own reward! What made you think of offering food, Michel, when you must have felt real fear?"

"The Lord seemed to press it into my mind," was Michel's simple explanation.

"Did you notice that he ate three servings?" Michel asked.

"I observed that," chuckled Heinrich. "With that huge

empty spot in his stomach, no wonder he felt mean when he showed up here!"

As the other emigrants trickled in from the Lehmann and Frei homes, they heard the story. No, they had not seen the man on horseback this morning.

Bernhard Lehmann led in prayer for the departing Swiss Brethren. He thanked the Lord who was a "very present help in trouble," for the protection He had given. Also, he prayed for the spiritual well being of the man on horseback.

After the Eggiwil brethren had showered the host families with many thanks, and the three families had promised prayers for the departing brothers and sisters, the emigrants started their united day's trek. Tucked among the comforters were love gifts of food, almost more than the emigrants could carry.

The bright sunlight, the distant mountains, the bronze, orange and amber leaves, the crisp fresh air, and most of all, the presence of God invigorated the brothers and sisters for the grueling journey toward Basel. What lay ahead? No one knew, but they were certain Who led them!

-EIGHTEEN -

A Night's Lodging

THE POSITIVE CONTACT WITH THE Kohlers, and then the Martins, Lehmanns, and Freis left a deep and satisfying impression on the hearts of the emigrants. Perhaps never again on this earth would they see those dear people. But the camaraderie and fellowship would live long in many of their memories.

The Swiss Brethren walked in silence, savoring the kindnesses they had received. They also remembered the Anabaptist hunter. Michel II, especially, felt a strange kinship with the needy man. Would he ever come to Christ?

Michel found himself praying for the man, but because he had no name for him, he decided to dub him "Oswald." Michel daily prayed for Oswald.

The plan was to walk beyond Balsthan and find a place to sleep. During the daytime, the sun became their friend, outdoing itself with brightness, although the air was quite nippy. As afternoon arrived, two scouts ran ahead to search out suitable lodging for the night.

About an hour's walk north of Balsthan they found a dilapidated and abandoned building. Then they ran back to the group.

"I have some details about our night's lodging," Peter Bachman reported. "The good news is that the place we found will cost us nothing because we saw no innkeeper. The bad news is that we observed plenty of ventilation, known as cracks in the walls, and rotten floor boards. Also, we saw no beds.

"Only the elderly, young families, and women are to have indoor lodging, as space is very limited. All of us scouts and some other men will need to sleep outside," he added matter-of-factly.

They arrived at their quarters as dusk was settling in. The temperature had dropped rapidly, and snow flurries powdered their heads.

"At least this dilapidated building provides a shelter of sorts," Anna told Michel, "but I feel so bad for those who need to sleep outside on a night like this," she shivered.

"I do, too," Michel sympathized. "But I'm going to offer to join them outside to make room for someone who needs to be inside more than I do."

But Peter Bachman objected when Michel offered. "Thank you," he said, "but you need to be inside with your wife and family."

During the night when Anna wakened, she was disoriented and unusually cold. In fact, her nose was very cold. In the darkness, she couldn't remember where she was. Then she heard a strange sound, "Scritch, scritch, scritch." Suddenly, it all came together, "No inn keeper and no bed," she thought. "The scratching sound must be rats!" she realized in horror as something flashed past her.

Otherwise all was still. The day's journey had been quite tiring, and it appeared that others slept in spite of the chilly temperature and the invasion of rats.

Before sunrise, the refugees stirred. The men who had slept outside came to the door and found floor seats when everyone was in a sitting position.

"Our Ana-baptist hunt-er would not be too a-mused if we of-fered him this morn-ing's cold break-fast fare," ventured scout Ulrich Stauffer, teeth chattering from the cold. "It's good he came yes-ter-day morn-ing."

"Nor would he have been excited about last night's outdoor lodging arrangement," offered red-nosed Hans Stauffer.

"Inside may have suited him better," volunteered Michel II, "where he could keep company with the rats!"

"I'm trying to decide if sharing nighttime quarters with deer, birds, wet leaves, and wind-blown snowflakes is better than lodging with rats," quipped Ulrich Liecte, rubbing his red nose.

After a general round of laughter, they all rose from their meager breakfast.

As Michael Schenk I prayed, their hearts were drawn to their heavenly Father, who really did care for them in this time of great uncertainty and need.

"Our Father in heaven," Michel began, "we hallow

Your name. Together we want to bring your Kingdom to our little part of the earth, and to do your will as long as You give us earthly life.

"Thank you for the food and the kind brothers and sisters who have shared with us in our time of need. Thank you for this humble place where we could rest.

"Help us to have forgiving hearts. Keep us from temptation of bitterness.

"For nothing can equal Your Kingdom, Your power, and Your glory.

"Guard the little ones among us, that they may in due time give their hearts to your service. May many generations to come follow in Your footsteps.

"For the Anabaptist hunter, we plead Your salvation. For the Martins, Lehmanns, and Freis, we ask peace; for the Kohlers, we plead grace and wisdom; for Ludwig we ask compassion as he showed it to us.

"Now as we follow You this day, please keep us from evil, strengthen us, and help us to show Christ to those we may meet. In the name of Jesus our Saviour, Amen."

The comforters were bundled on backs, the door to the aged building was shut behind them, and the trek of a new day began.

The city of Basel. They were headed to the wonder city of Basel!

When Anna was fourteen, her cousin Barbara's family had visited a family in Basel. Barbara had returned to Eggiwil with marvelous tales of the glamorous city.

At the time, Anna was quite jealous. As Barbara sat

describing the elegant and stately homes along the street where their hosts lived, her lively chatter stirred a desire in Anna's heart that she had never known before.

"Eggiwil does look quite simple and dull," sighed Barbara on that day long ago. "We slept in fine canopy beds with beautiful curtains at the windows. We could see the majestic blue waters of the Rhine River from our windows. The shops were filled with all sorts of lovely gifts, clothing and other items to buy. And the food was amazing!" she rolled her eyes. "There's no place quite like it," sighed Barbara again, as if she had visited all the world's most glamorous cities, and Basel topped them all.

Anna had punctuated Barbara's chatter with 'oh' and 'ah' at appropriate times, but her frame of reference was miniscule in contrast to Barbara's now-cosmopolitan knowledge.

As the emigrants stopped and ate lunch on this sunny, brisk day, Anna found herself sitting next to Margareta Roet.

"Margareta, have you ever visited Basel?"

Margareta looked shocked that Anna should ask such a question. "Why no! Have you, Anna?"

Anna laughed, "No, I haven't. But my cousin, Barbara, was there when she was fourteen. She and I are the same age, so when she returned to simple, dull, Eggiwil, I soaked up her marvelous tales of the city."

Anna continued, "Their hosts took them to the ancient Martinskirche for Sunday service, and they toured the beautiful Basel Minster. They stayed along a street with elegant and lovely homes. They went shopping on Freie Street where charming shops sell beautiful clothing and exquisite gifts. Ladies in fashionable dresses strolled Middle Bridge."

Margareta sat wide-eyed as Anna rattled on. "Oh, Margareta, I was fourteen, very impressionable, and had not yet yielded my life to Christ. All this charm was held, like a sparkling gem, beyond my grasp!"

"Now I finally get to go to Basel," Anna continued, "And do you know what? My highest priority for my time in Basel is for our group to move safely in and out of the wonder city!"

Margareta rolled her eyes and nodded in agreement, "We certainly don't care about all the city's beautiful treasures if the officials lock us up in prison!" she responded dramatically.

"For all its splendor, Basel did not appreciate some of the earlier Anabaptists," Anna said solemnly. "Let's pray that the city will let us depart its boundary in peace!"

"Oh yes, let's pray!" Margareta nodded vigorously.

–NINETEEN–

Ludwig and Johannes

ULRICH STAUFFER AND HANS STAUFFER walked ahead of the group to find lodging for the night. Walking with great strides, they hoped to find an adequate place and return to the slow-moving caravan so that everyone could arrive at the quarters before dusk.

As they walked, many of the refugees were praying that the Stauffer men could find adequate lodging. If it turned as bitter as it had the night before and *everyone* had to sleep outside . . .

Anna noticed how the October sun glinted on the white-haired men ahead of her. Christian Stauffer, about ninety years old, relied on his cane. But Anna thought her grandpapa managed amazingly well for his age.

Her husband's uncle, Christian Schenk, at age ninety-five, was the oldest of the emigrants. He also did very well on the journey. His desire to serve the Lord was still strong.

And then there was Michel Schenk I, who seemed to have bounced back well from his affliction. He and his older brother, Christian, each had a tall, dignified bearing.

Anna could not help but deeply appreciate these aged men who were determined to stay true to Christ regardless of the cost. What an example of faithfulness they were to younger family members. Their days on earth were numbered, yet they were willing to sacrifice themselves physically for the sake of Christ.

"Lord, give us this day our daily bread and our nightly lodging," Anna pleaded, as her weary body plodded forward. Last night's rest had been punctuated with wakefulness and shivery temperatures.

As the group tramped through a wooded area, two riders appeared on horseback.

"Friends or foes?" thought Anna, her heart thumping.

Michel II grasped little Michel a little more tightly and drew closer to Anna and the other children.

"Where would your group of people be going?" asked one rider, pleasantly.

Peter Bachman spoke up, "Basel."

"Basel?" the rider queried. "Do you expect . . . do you plan to arrive by nightfall?"

"I think not," Peter replied.

"So where do you plan to go before arriving at Basel?"

"We hope to use an abandoned building for nighttime quarters, sir," Peter replied politely.

"If that is the case, you may use my barn for the night,"

offered the stranger.

"Sir, that is quite fine of you to offer. . ."

"I'm sure you are welcome," the rider stated simply. "We live on the way to Basel. Just continue northward while we attend to our errand, and soon we shall be back."

The refugees looked around in awe, smiling. A barn for the night! Freely offered! The Lord had provided.

While the man and his son were gone, the group gathered for a brief prayer of thanks, then continued on their way, hoping that Ulrich and Hans Stauffer would soon return.

In about an hour, the man and his son returned to the emigrants. "My name is Melcher Hess, and this is my son, Isaak. I will send Isaak on ahead to tell my other family members you are coming, and one of you may go with him, riding my horse. I will walk with the rest of you to show you the way."

Peter Bachman had done a lot of horseback riding, so he was the logical choice to take Melcher's horse.

As the group walked, Anna could see that scout Ulrich Liecte and Melcher talked animatedly, but she couldn't hear the discussion.

When they arrived at the Hess home, Melcher's wife, Lucia, met them smiling. "What a treat it is to have guests!"

The children politely introduced themselves in order of age: Bernhard, Isaak, Susanna, Katharina, Georg, and Hans.

"The girls have helped me prepare, so we should be able to eat in about an hour," Lucia announced cheerfully.

"Where are Ulrich and Hans Stauffer?" questioned Peter Bachman.

"Oh yes, they were searching for an overnight place for us. . ." Ulrich Liecte said. "I'll go out to the path and see if I can spot them returning."

After an hour, Ulrich Liecte came in with Ulrich and Hans Stauffer.

"We found a place," Hans announced, "but we weren't excited about the accommodation. The building was smaller and more drafty than the last one. But thanks to Melcher's family and their barn, we shall fare quite well."

The Hess family was as hospitable as any of the other families had been. Their barn was snug, and their food was ample.

Furthermore, they had deep compassion for the Anabaptists. "I knew you must be leaving the land to avoid persecution," Melcher told the emigrants. "Why else would a large group be tramping through the woods headed for Basel? We want you to know we believe everyone should have the freedom to practice their faith according to their conscience."

The Hess family persuaded them to stay a few days and to rest up and eat well before heading down the Rhine at Basel.

Peter Bachman and Ulrich Liecte set out early the following morning for Basel. They needed to check out available ship travel down the Rhine.

When they returned that evening, Peter's eyes were bright with excitement. "We stepped into a shop on Freie

Street, where I wanted to purchase a little food for us to eat," he reported. "I was standing behind another customer waiting to ask for the cheese I wanted. A previous customer had laid two Reichsthaler on the counter in payment for his food. While the shop keeper had his back turned, I saw a hand reach out and stealthily grasp the coins. Then the thief quickly mingled with the crowd in the shop, but he was making his way toward the door. When the shop keeper turned around, his money was gone. He immediately turned on the customer waiting in front of me.

"'Who do you think you are, common thief? Do you think you can steal money from me and get by with it'? His face turned livid."

"The man in front of me turned his head slightly, helpless to prove his innocence against such an onslaught. And I recognized him as Ludwig Kohler, the constable!"

"'Sir', I calmly addressed the shop keeper, 'this was not the man who took your two Reichsthaler.'"

"'Here is the thief', someone cried out, dragging forward the petty robber, who still clutched the coins in his hand."

"'Get the constable', yelled the shop keeper. So someone hurried out for the constable, and a couple other men pinned the thief against the wall. Meanwhile, the shop keeper distractedly waited on Ludwig and then me. When Ulrich and I left the shop, Ludwig was outside waiting for us."

"'Thanks for stating my innocence', Ludwig said."

"'Of course', I told him. 'Even if I hadn't seen the other man take the money, I wouldn't have believed you were a thief'."

"'So what brings you to Basel'? I asked."

"'I'm visiting my elderly mama. After arriving here I learned that she is in poor health, and that this may be the last time I see her alive'. His eyes clouded."

"'I'm sorry to hear that, Ludwig. We will pray for your mama. I will tell the other brothers and sisters, too'."

"'Thank you so much', he told me. He even said, 'You may pray for me, too. I would like to know Christ as you do'."

"'Why Ludwig, we will be happy to do that', I told him."

"'I must be going now', he announced abruptly and was off."

"Ulrich will tell you who we met later," Peter said.

"We went to the wharf," Ulrich began, "to inquire about a ship for our travel to the Palatinate, in German territory, and we found a most interesting contact. We met a man by the name of Johannes Bachmann. Do any of you remember his papa, Niklaus Bachmann, who lived in the area of Knubel, Eggiwil?"

Michel I's eyes lit up, "Yes, I do!"

"Niklaus Bachmann was ill for about a year before he died," continued Ulrich.

"Johannes was young when that happened, and while Niklaus was ill, Michel I many times helped with farm work, especially during hay cutting. Michel II went along, and he and Johannes worked like little men. Then their papas gave them a bit of playtime," explained Ulrich.

Michel II's eyes were glowing, "We had wonderful times together. He was one of my best friends as a boy!"

"He felt the same way about you, Michel," Ulrich said.

"But after his papa died," Ulrich continued, "the work became too much for Johannes and his mama. Johannes had dreamed of becoming a ship captain, so they moved to Basel for him to learn the craft of sailing. He begged us to let him take us on his ship *The Alpen Blue*."

– TWENTY –

The Alpen Blue

ON THE MORNING OF DEPARTURE, THE refugees ate a warm breakfast prepared by Lucia and her daughters. Food packets also were prepared for needed meals on the journey.

With heartfelt thanks to their host family, the refugees set out for their trip to Basel and down the Rhine River on *The Alpen Blue*.

Michel II confided to Anna, "I'm quite excited to see Johannes after all these years! But what will it be like to bridge the gap between boyhood and manhood? I wonder if he is married and has children. And if his mama is still living. I remember Johannes had stars in his eyes when he dreamed of someday sailing on the Rhine."

"I'm so excited for you to see Johannes again, too! Who would have dreamed that this would come about on our journey to the new land? What special evidences we've had that God cares about our needs and our happiness!"

When they arrived at the harbor, Michel spotted Johannes. He quickly took his family to meet his boyhood friend. "Johannes! It's been a long time since we worked and played together on your papa's farm at Knubel!"

Johannes looked with curiosity at the man who spoke to him, then recognition flew into his eyes. "Michel!" he exclaimed. "I heard you were on the way. This is a most amazing coincidence! No, not coincidence—because I believe that God planned for us to meet!

"And is this your family?" Johannes asked with interest.

"Yes, this is my wife, Anna; my son Christian is nine years old; Hans is six; Barbara is four; and Michel III is going on two years old."

"What a fine family you have, Michel! Amazing, how the years rolled by and here we both are with wives and children!"

When Michel I stepped out of the shadows, he said, "My son, Johannes! You look so much like your papa! How could we ever have expected to meet like this?" The old man's eyes shone.

"May I call you Papa?" queried Johannes. "And thank you for the way you blessed our family in our time of need many years ago."

"Certainly you may call me Papa. I wish I could have done more . . ."

When the emigrants tried to pay fare for the voyage, Captain Bachmann politely declined to take any money. "The fare was paid forward many years ago," he explained. "Michel Schenk I had a heart of gold and helped my family when my papa was sick. Michel II helped, too, and he and I became fast friends. Finally, I have a chance to do a favor in return."

The emigrants hardly knew how to thank Captain Bachmann for such kindness, but they expressed their gratitude the best they could.

Only when they were sailing far down the Rhine did Anna think about what the city of Basel had done for her. Their group had been able to move safely in and out of the 'wonder city'! Much as she had valued her homeland, it was a huge relief to feel free from the threat of potential Anabaptist hunters and a possible prison lock up. Now they were setting their faces toward a new land and a new life.

Michel II noticed that his son Christian stayed by his side while he talked with Johannes. Ordinarily, Christian would be curious about all the interesting sights to see as they sailed down river. But he was gratified that Christian valued listening to the conversation more than seeing the scenery.

"Do you remember when we played together on the slopes?" Johannes asked. "First, we raced *uphill*."

"That often ended in a tie," Michel remembered. "But the racing *downhill* turned into a disaster for me!" He shook his head and laughed heartily. "On one occasion I guess I stumbled over my feet. Anyway, I went ker-splat on the ground. Of course, you easily won that race. In fact, every time I raced downhill after that, I was afraid of going headfirst to the ground, and you flew past me like a light-footed deer!"

Christian was laughing, "Papa, I would have liked to see you go ker-splat!"

"Remember the time we hid from our papas, and your papa called our names many times, ringing a cowbell over and over?" Johannes asked. "But we wanted to keep the game going for awhile, so we stayed hidden. When we finally saw your papa give up in defeat, we came out from our hiding place grinning. But your papa didn't grin. Instead he wore a dark cloud on his face. He told us to go and apologize to my papa, who, of course, was very sick at that time."

"That's not the end of the story," Michel said ruefully. "When Papa and I went home, he caused me to be *very* sorry for what I had done! Ouch!"

"Did you get a spanking, Papa?" Christian's eyes were large with wonder and dismay.

"Yes, my son, I got a spanking worthy of the name! My papa correctly guessed that it was my idea to hide and then stay hidden. That was bad enough. But Johannes' papa was a very sick man who didn't need the stress this caused. My papa knew that we were young boys who didn't understand the stress involved for parents. But he also knew that he needed to teach us never to repeat a prank like that.

"And I never did," Michel II added.

"Remember the time we went to Eggiwil for medicine for my papa?" Johannes asked.

"Yes, we felt very grown up. We tried no tricks that

time!" Michel remembered.

"My papa died not too long after that," Johannes recalled. "But before his death, he told me very seriously to take care of my mama. I promised him I would do that. My mama still lives with us.

"Do you remember that our farm was sold after Papa died? The farmer who bought it was a kind man and let us live in the house while he farmed the fields. I helped him with farm work. He bought some of our cows, too. But we kept three cows, which mama milked. She made cheese, and I took most of it to the village to sell."

Michel nodded, "Yes, I remember going with you to the village and helping you take cheese."

Johannes turned to Christian, "I keep looking at your face, Christian, and there I see your papa of long ago. He was a healthy-looking boy with rosy checks, too. He also had blue-gray eyes and dark brown hair."

Christian smiled and nodded.

"Did you know I married Elsbeth Eymann?" Johannes asked Michel.

"No, when you moved to Basel, I completely lost track of you."

"I didn't want to marry a girl from Basel," Johannes explained. "But I remembered Elsbeth and made some trips back to Eggiwil to see her before we got married. Now we have two sons. Niklaus, named after my papa, is ten."

Christian's eyes lit up and he smiled, "He's a bit older than I am."

"Your papa told me your age. I believe he said you are

nine," said Johannes.

"Yes, I'm nine," Christian answered.

"You are a fine young man, Christian," Johannes commented.

Christian thought, "There it is again—*young man.*"

But he just said, "Thank you, Captain Bachmann."

"My son Michel is eight. He was named after *your* Papa, Christian," Johannes said.

"Oh!" Christian clapped his hand over his mouth, then grinned and looked at his papa.

Michel II smiled and said quietly, "That's quite an honor, Johannes."

The Lord's Day found the group collected on deck for a brief service.

Elderly Christian Stauffer spoke from Hebrews 13:5-8, "Let your conversation be without covetousness; and be content with such things as ye have: for he hath said, I will never leave thee, nor forsake thee. So that we may boldly say, The Lord is my helper, and I will not fear what man shall do unto me. Remember them which have the rule over you, who have spoken unto you the word of God: whose faith follow, considering the end of their conversation. Jesus Christ the same yesterday, and to day, and for ever."

Christian spoke simply from their own experience. "When we started this trip, we had no way of knowing what lay ahead, but we knew we journeyed with Jesus!

"Our heavenly Father watched over us as we walked, protected us as we slept on the ground, delivered us from

Anabaptist hunter, provided the Jakob Kohler family, supplied the Martin, Lehmann, and Frei families, and then provided the Hess family. Now the Lord is using our wonderful Captain Bachmann to take us down the Rhine!

"The Lord truly has been faithful to His promise, never to leave us nor forsake us . . 'The Lord is my helper, and I will not fear what man shall do unto me'. As we have experienced God's faithfulness in this recent past, so we know *He* will never leave us in the future.

"But surpassing the physical benefits that have blessed us on our way, however, is the promise, 'Jesus Christ the same yesterday, and to day, and for ever'. The salvation, brotherhood, grace, mercy, and peace that are ours through Him transcend all earthly treasures."

After prayer, Michel II led in a hymn:

"Rejoice, rejoice, ye Christians all,
and break forth into singing!
Since far and wide on ev'ry side
the Word of God is ringing.
And well ye know, no human foe
Our souls from Christ can sever;
For to the base and men of grace,
God's Word stands sure forever."

Then Captain Bachmann spoke briefly, "These words in Isaiah 46 should encourage the elderly among you," Johannes said. "'And even to your old age I am he; and even to hoar hairs will I carry you: I have made and I will bear; even I will carry, and will deliver you.'"

Johannes continued, "I have been blessed and encouraged to see men and women of God, including the very elderly, willing to sacrifice and step into the unknown for their faith in Christ. I want to speak a particular blessing to Michel Schenk I for the way he and his son helped on our farm in our time of need many years ago. Little did I dream then that the Lord would bring us together in this way years later!"

– TWENTY-ONE –

The Lord Is My Shepherd ... Through the Valley

AFTER DISEMBARKING FROM *THE Alpen Blue,* the Swiss Brethren went first to the Dirmstein in the Palatinate and eventually settled at Ibersheimer Hof at Osthofen. By the early part of 1672, the Eggiwil Brethren had been counted among over six hundred people who left their Swiss homeland and headed for the Palatinate. The Palatinate ruler welcomed Anabaptists, in an effort to have farmers to build up this land, ruined in the Thirty Years' War.

Two Anabaptist brethren, Valentin Huetwol and Juryaen Liechte, conducted a census of Anabaptists who had immigrated to the Palatinate. The need for material help was great among these immigrants.

God graciously supplied aid through the kindness of

honorable men in the Netherlands. The city of Amsterdam was the hub for this organized relief program.

The Swiss Brethren reminded each other, "Has not God promised, 'I will never leave thee, nor forsake thee.'" Their gratitude toward the generous Dutch and their all-sufficient God knew no bounds.

The day came when Michel Schenk I knew that his time on earth was nearly finished.

"Papa," Michel II told him, "thank you for the wonderful example of godliness you have been to me. I love you and will miss you so much. But let me encourage you with these words from Scripture,

'I have fought a good fight, I have finished my course, I have kept the faith: Henceforth there is laid up for me a crown of righteousness, which the Lord, the righteous judge, shall give me at that day: and not to me only, but to all them also that love his appearing'."

"Michel, you have been a kind and faithful son," said the elderly man. "My cup of love for you is full."

Christian's eyes were big when he told his grandpapa goodbye. "Grandpapa, remember that day when I told you, 'Please don't die yet'. I'm so glad God let you live for a while. But now, if Jesus is calling you to come to Him, that's all right. I'll always think of you with love," he said as his eyes brimmed with tears.

"My young man, I hold you close to my heart with

love," Grandpapa said, "When God calls you, please give your heart completely to Jesus and help to build His Kingdom."

Michel II and Christian listened carefully as Michel I breathed the words, "The Lord is my Shepherd ... through the valley."

Epilogue

*I*N THE SUMMER OF 1717, CHRISTIAN Schenk stood on the deck of a ship headed west across the Atlantic Ocean to America.

Ocean spray misted his face, and salt tingled his skin. He tasted the tang when he licked his lips.

Perhaps one more week would bring this floating crowd of Mennists into the harbor in Philadelphia. These Swiss/German Palantines were headed to the land of hope and promise.

Though the Palantine ruler had granted the immigrants limited religious freedom, still hardships had been intense.

In the War of the Grand Alliance (1688-1697), the French king, Louis XIV's troops caused much devastation in the land.

A new Palantine ruler came to power in 1716. High fees and other difficulties in the Palatinate prompted these Mennists to find relocation very appealing when urged by pioneer settler Martin Kendig to join the group already in Pennsylvania.

"Sailing on an ocean voyage is not something most people would do for adventure," thought Christian ruefully. Food rations consisted of thin soup and hard, sometimes wormy, bread. The three ships carried a total of three hundred and sixty-three passengers. The holds were crammed, and unpleasant odors lingered. Many of Christian's fellow passengers were now below deck struggling with seasickness.

Christian thought about his place in life now. His dear wife, Barbara, had passed on to a better home three years before. His three sons and three daughters were traveling with him: Anna, Michael, Margaret, Heinrich, Barbara, and Jacob. Michael's young wife, Mary, was along, too.

Benedikt Brechbühl was leader of this group of immigrants to Pennsylvania. Christian's late wife, Barbara, had been Benedikt's sister. So the two men planned to purchase land together shortly after they arrived.

As Christian stood on the deck, he suddenly sensed a presence nearby. Turning, he saw Michael and Mary.

"How long do you think the voyage will take yet?" Michael queried.

"According to Captain, about a week," Christian said.

"I was thinking of many years ago," Christian continued, "when Papa, Mama, Grandpapa, Hans, Barbara, little Michel and I made our journey to the Palatinate. I was nine and quite ripe for adventure. We *had* some adventures, too. Michael, you know some of the stories!

"But I did not fully understand what leaving their

homeland meant to my parents and to my grandpapa. We took practically nothing along. Just two comforters and a little money.

Michael remarked, "I remember your papa and mama as kind and sincere grandparents. They had made their peace with Christ, and they had made their peace with life, it seemed. Regardless of the difficulties they had faced, they took it in stride. Their highest aim was to honor Christ."

"Yes, I was truly blessed to have such godly parents. I remember something my papa said in his prayer before we left Eggiwil for the Palatinate.

"He said, 'I believe this is a journey of destiny'. Because of my parents' decision to live by their convictions and thus leave the land, he believed his children and future generations could be influenced by that. He prayed that God would stir the hearts of ongoing generations to take their own steps of faith for Christ and His Kingdom."

Michael and Mary nodded solemnly.

Here are excerpts from a Baccalaureate Address given in 1973 by Byard W. Shank, who was an eleventh generation descendant from Michel Schenk I:

The Bible says, "NEGLECT NOT THE GIFT THAT IS IN THEE."

I believe that God has given a special gift or ability to each of us. I believe that God has a purpose for each person that he can better fulfill than anyone else. God intends that we use this gift to glorify Him and make life brighter for our fellowmen.

I am jealous of your privilege to live in this day.
I have had my day. Today is your day.

I believe it is a wonderful time to be young;
not because life will be easy,
not because temptations will be less,
not because your earthly future is bright.
But because all of this presents to you a marvelous opportunity to magnify the grace of God in this your day!
You are living and serving now! TODAY!
If you are projecting yourself into tomorrow, you are losing today.
Don't wait for opportunities;
you have them today!
The world will be a little poorer if you neglect your gift.

The world will be a little darker
*   if you do not let your light shine.*

I commend to you the Christian life,
*   the born-of-God life.*
*   It is the only life of peace,*
*   the only life of joy,*
*   the only life of satisfaction,*
*   the only life of hope,*
*   the only life that has promise of eternal reward.*

Go as men and women, confident that God has
a purpose for each of you, knowing that as you
are born of God and submit to His leading; these
purposes will be fulfilled in your lives.

Go as lights, with the awareness that unless God's
light shines through the youth of our generation,
then it will go out in your generation. Then it will be
dark—exceedingly dark!

I challenge you to become the children of God
*   Through the life of Jesus Christ in you.*

I challenge you to give your lives in service to
your generation under the Lordship of Jesus Christ.

AND MAY GOD BLESS YOU!
AMEN

Schenk-Shank Family Ancestry

BORN*	ANCESTOR	SPOUSE	BORN*
~1470	Hans Schenk		
~1505	Johannes Schenk	Elsbeth Neuenschander	1510
~1530	Johannes Christian Schenk	Margareth Wenger	
~1564	Ulrich Schenk	Annali Rytz	
~1590	Michael Schenk I	Anna Stauffer	
~1639	Michael Schenk II	Anna Stauffer	1643
~1662	Christian Stauffer Schenk	Barbara Brechbüll	1673
~1692	Michael Schenk	Mary	1695
~1718	Michael Schenk	Magdalena	1720
~1758	Henry Shank	Anna (Ann) Reiff	1761
~1787	Henry Shank	Elizabeth Heatwole	1792
~1819	Jacob Shank	Mary Driver	1824
~1847	Daniel Peter Shank	Mary Catherine Ruff	1849
~1873	James Henry Shank	Lydia Frances Lahman	1875
~1918	Byard Wenger Shank	Anna Ruth Hertzler	1914
~1949	Patricia Louise Shank	John Diller Martin	1946

*Dates are approximates

Fact, Fiction, or Maybe So
(and some sources)

Most of the narrative in *A Journey of Destiny* is fiction. However, the backbone of the story is true: Michel Schenk I, Michel II and his wife Anna, with their children Christian, Hans, Barbara, and Michel III left Canton Bern in the Swiss Confederation, headed for the Palatinate in Germany, in the year 1671.

Preface – "Michel Schenk" is the spelling used in *History of the Bernese Anabaptists*. I used the labels Michel I, Michel II, and Michel III, which I read on an internet source, as a means of easy identification.

Map – Even though Switzerland didn't become a country (federal state) until September 12, 1848, prior to that a confederation of cantons held together some of the territory we now know as Switzerland. The term Switzerland is used on the map. Germany consisted of independent states at this time in history.

I don't know what route the emigrants followed to reach the Palatinate.

Prologue – The genealogy of Hans, Johannes, Johannes Christian, Ulrich, Michel (I), Michel (II), and Christian Schenk, I have received from my brother, Ray Shank. I assumed they all lived in the Emmental, which is the valley of the Emme River.

Chapter One – "The date was October 16, 1671." I based this date upon the minister's written testimony of October 16 that Eggiwil's Täufer had left. (Although they may have left on one of the previous days.) This information was taken from *History of the Bernese Anabaptists*, Pathway Publishers, page 374.

The terms "papa," and "mama," used in this chapter and throughout the story are the titles used for parents because of the explanation given in *History of the Bernese Anabaptists,* on page 140. An Anabaptist was asked what parents should be called since the term "father" was not to be used (as Jesus instructs in Matthew 23:9 that it refers only to God). Children should refer to their parents as "Poppa," (I used the colloquial spelling "Papa,"); "Momma," ("Mama").

Chapter Two – Georg and Elsbeth Egli are entirely fictitious characters. These are first and last names, however, that appear in *History of the Bernese Anabaptists*. I often paired up a first name from one place with a last name from another place that were mentioned in the above book.

Chapter Three – Anna remembered the christening dates of her children. These were likely the dates recorded in the Eggiwil Reformed Church registry. But were these the christening dates? or the actual birthdates of the babies?

I believe it is true that Christian Stauffer was Anna Stauffer Schenk's paternal grandpapa.

The Hans Roet and Hans Schneider families were among those mentioned in the book *History of the Bernese Anabaptists* as staying at Osthofen, Palatinate, along with the Schenks early in 1672, I "assigned" them also as fellow travelers of the Schenks from Eggiwil. Their wives' names were not given, I assigned their names as well as Margareta (Roet) and Katharina (Schneider).

Hans Roet and Hans Schneider were actual people, so it is not redundant to use the name Hans more than once. However, later in the story I assigned names for fictitious characters. If someone thinks I overused the name "Hans," please be advised that the index of *History of the Bernese Anabaptists* lists over one hundred fifty men with the name Hans! (Granted, in the confusion of various languages or even dialects referenced, etc., overlaps of individuals may have occurred.) However, suffice it to say, Hans was an extremely popular name in this era!

All of the following names are used to describe the group of people in this story: Anabaptists; Swiss Brethren; refugees; emigrants (when they were *leaving* Swiss territory; immigrants (when they *arrived* in German territory).

Chapter Four – The elderly Christian Schenk, who was ninety-five years old, was mentioned in this story as Anna's husband's uncle (a brother to Michel I). *The Mennonite Encyclopedia, copyright 1959, Vol. IV, page 509,* leaves it a question whether Michel I and Christian were brothers.

Chapter Five – "The Ulrich Eymann family had brought with them a cow, named *Gentle...*" is quoted from chapter five in this story. In the book *History of the Bernese Anabaptists,* (page 65) Ulrich Eymann and his wife and child were real people. They were among those staying at Ibersheimer Hof, Osthofen, in the Palatinate, along with the Schenks and others. A cow was listed among their possessions. I named her *Gentle.*

Chapter Ten – Even though the Jakob Kohler family I mention is fictitious, the Anabaptist escape tunnel at a home in the Sumiswald area is real. See the photo section. I got to step inside the tunnel. Our daughter and son-in-law, Candace and Heinrich Schander, explored the narrow tunnel pretty well to the end (it is not as long as the original tunnel because it collapsed at the end, we were told). The gracious lady of the house let Heinrich, Candace, John and me come into this remarkable house.

At first, Anabaptists could escape through the tunnel and into a forest. The Anabaptist hunters could not arrest them because the forest was in a different district from the house under which they escaped. However, later that "escape" no longer applied, and they could be caught.

Many citizens sympathized with the Anabaptists and did not agree with punishing them for their faith. These people were Anabaptist sympathizers or half-Anabaptists. The Jakob Kohler family represents this group of citizens.

Chapter Eleven – Christian Stauffer apparently was imprisoned at Thun Castle in 1644, according to an internet source. One flimsy little account has my ancestor (referred to as Jacob Stauffer instead of Christian Stauffer) escaping from a castle in Thun when he was about 90 years of age. Did Christian escape? We don't know.

History of the Bernese Anabaptists, page 223, spells the last name of Christian, his son Ulrich, and his grandson Hans, *Stauffert.* I used the spelling Stauffer.

Chapter Twenty-one – It appears that Michel Schenk I passed away in 1672, if my internet source is accurate.

Epilogue / Schenk – Shank Ancestry – It appears from one or more of these sources that Christian Schenk had three sons and three daughters. Also, perhaps some birth dates were taken from these sources.

There may be inaccuracies among some of the earliest ancestors listed.

Posted on (copyright) Geni, from George Shank's research: THE SHANKS FAMILY OF PEQUEA CREEK by J. Arthur Shanks, 205 S. Broadway, Providence, KY. Repository: The Lancaster Mennonite Historical Society, 2215 Millstream Road, Lancaster, PA 17602-1499; Phone (717)393-9745; also Daniel Haster, Ibersheim (Reinland-Pfalz, Germany) Global Anabaptist Mennonite Encyclopedia.

SOURCES: Some sources of information for this story were: *History of the Bernese Anabaptists,* copyright 2010, Pathway Publishers, Alymer, ON, LaGrange, IN. German edition by Ernst Müller, English translation by John A. Gingerich; Richard W. Davis ? (Schenk family genealogist, trickle down information through one or more sources); various internet sources; *The Mennonite Encyclopedia,* copyright 1959, Vol. IV, page 509; (copyright) Geni, from George Shank's research: THE SHANKS FAMILY OF PEQUEA CREEK by J. Arthur Shanks, 205 S. Broadway, Providence, KY. Repository: The Lancaster Mennonite Historical Society, 2215 Millstream Road, Lancaster, PA 17602-1499; Phone (717)393-9745; also Daniel Haster, Ibersheim (Reinland-Pfalz, Germany) Global Anabaptist Mennonite Encyclopedia. *The World Book Encyclopedia, (So-Sz), Volume 18, 1999 Edition; The World Book Encyclopedia (G), Volume 8, 1999 Edition,* provided names of towns and rivers.

About the author

Patricia Shank Martin has long been fascinated with biographies. Often Christian biographies reveal people honed by hardship to accomplish the will of God. Patricia is humbly grateful to be the descendant of one such man of God, Michel Schenk I.

She is the daughter of the late Byard and Anna Ruth Shank. Following her stint as a school teacher, she was an office secretary at Christian Light Publications. She married John D. Martin in 1979, and they are the parents of four living children and the grandparents of nine living grandchildren.